Praise for Robert Goldsborough
THREE STRIKES YOU'RE DEAD

"Goldsborough, best known as the heir to Rex Stout via his half-dozen Nero Wolfe novels, creates a prewar Chicago that is at once sinister and appealing. He also weaves an engaging subplot involving Dizzy Dean and the Chicago Cubs' drive to the 1938 World Series. An enormously entertaining caper." –Wes Lukowsky, *Booklist* 100th Anniversary Issue

"Robert Goldsborough, the man who so brilliantly brought Rex Stout's Nero Wolfe and Archie Goodwin back to literary life, has returned with a new detective, all his own – and that's cause for any mystery fan to rejoice! Goldsborough is a master storyteller, providing crackling dialogue and plot twists around every corner – readers are in for a real treat!" –Max Allan Collins, author of *Road to Purgatory*

MURDER IN E MINOR

"Goldsborough has not only written a first-rate mystery that stands on its own merits, he has faithfully re-created the round detective and his milieu." –PHILADELPHIA ENQUIRER

"Mr. Goldsborough has all of the late writer's stylistic mannerisms down pat." –THE NEW YORK TIMES on *Murder in E Minor*

"A smashing success…" –CHICAGO SUN-TIMES

"A half dozen other writers have attempted it, but Goldsborough's is the only one that feels authentic, the only one able to get into Rex's psyche. If I hadn't known otherwise, I might have been fooled into thinking this was the genius Stout myself." –John McAleer, Rex Stout's official biographer and editor of *The Stout Journal*

ALSO BY ROBERT GOLDSBOROUGH

SNAP MALEK MYSTERIES FROM ECHELON PRESS

THREE STRIKES YOU'RE DEAD

NERO WOLFE MYSTERIES FROM BANTAM BOOKS

MURDER IN E MINOR

DEATH ON DEADLINE

FADE TO BLACK

THE BLOODIED IVY

THE LAST COINCIDENCE

SILVER SPIRE

THE MISSING CHAPTER

Robert Goldsborough

Shadow of the Bomb

A Snap Malek Mystery

Echelon Press
Publishing

SHADOW OF THE BOMB

A Snap Malek Mystery

Book Two

An Echelon Press Book

First Echelon Press paperback printing / October 2006

Echelon Press

9735 Country Meadows Lane 1-D

Laurel, MD 20723

www.echelonpress.com

ISBN 1-59080-491-0

Library of Congress Control Number: 2006928244

PRINTED IN THE UNITED STATES OF AMERICA

10 9 8 7 6 5 4 3 2 1

To my good friend Marvin Green, whose experiences as a University of Chicago student in 1942 suggested this tale.

Chicago

Prologue

Lord, he was exhausted. This had been his longest day yet in what he had come to call "the basement." When he finally got out, he was too tired to even drop in at the U.T. for a nightcap. The unrelenting deadline pressure was bad enough, but the damn secrecy made it even worse.

It seemed like everybody he knew on the faculty was asking questions, always more questions. He knew many of them were jealous, of course. That was obvious–and understandable. But he couldn't go anywhere now without the probing, nosing, snooping.

"What is it you're *really* working on?" became the standard opening query, and when he gave his stock reply about it being "just a metallurgy lab project," he got the eye rolls, tongue-clucking, and arch comments, such as, "Yeah, sure, that's why we never see you in your office." "That's why you're not teaching now." "That's why so many buildings on the campus are boarded up, with those armed soldiers out in front–even at poor old Stagg Field, for God's sake." "Don't give us that met lab crap. Something big's going on, isn't it?"

He wanted to scream, "Yes, dammit, something big *is* going on, the biggest thing that's ever happened in the history of warfare, and it's happening right under your prying noses. End of discussion–now leave me alone."

But of course, such behavior was out of the question– even though on a couple of occasions he had told some strangers at the U.T. bar that they need not be concerned about how the war would ultimately end. That at least stopped their whining about the pounding we were taking in the Pacific and Europe. But he knew he had to avoid that kind of reaction from now on. And maybe he should also stop hanging around the U.T. for awhile.

He was almost sorry that he had been one of the chosen. But then, he was all too aware of his own brilliance and would have taken great offense if he'd been left out. At first, it was both exciting and patriotic, being a part of history. But now, after the long days and sometimes nights in that dank, gray, windowless pit under the old grandstands, the excitement had morphed into tedium, and each day he felt himself to be an ever-smaller part of history.

True, it was a privilege being around the likes of Fermi and Szilard and other physicists whom he admired, some almost to the point of hero-worship. But his role was so small, and they tended to look down upon him–he could feel it, even though nothing ever was said.

Well, he was home now. He pressed his palms against his eyes and lay his head down on the desk, almost too tired to go into the bedroom and pull on his pajamas.

The knock startled him, but then he figured it must be that garrulous old spinster down the hall, come to borrow of cup of sugar, or maybe flour. She seemed to always be running out of something, although more likely it was an excuse to chat. She was lonesome, although he wished she would find someone else to chatter to about the weather or her leaky kitchen faucet or her darling twin nieces in Topeka or her alcoholic brother up on the North Side who was always asking her for money.

"Well, this is quite a surprise," he said as he pulled open the door. "I didn't hear the buzzer."

"I didn't have to use it," his visitor replied with a thin smile. "Somebody was just leaving and held the door for me down in the foyer. Very nice of him. I happened to be in the neighborhood, and I thought you wouldn't mind my dropping by. So this is your place? Pleasant. Hope I'm not catching you at a bad time," the visitor said, stepping inside without waiting for an answer.

"No, not at all, I just didn't expect you–or anybody else, for that matter. Yes, this is simple though comfortable, like I think I've mentioned to you before. Small but efficient kitchen, and as you can see, plenty of room for a desk, which I refer to as my off-campus office," he said, gesturing to a corner of the living room. "And in there is the bedroom." He pivoted and turned his back to his visitor. "Can I get you something to–"

What came next was child's play–akin to a steer being roped by a veteran cowpoke. In an instant, the looped and knotted cord dropped over his head. He got his hands under the garrote as it tightened around his neck, but it was too late to even yell.

He thrashed about, gasping and grasping, as the struggle moved across the living room in the direction of the bedroom. His visitor had the element of surprise and the leverage, however, steadily increasing the pressure. He tried to retaliate, jabbing backwards ineffectively with one elbow and then the other. In desperation, he lunged in an attempt to break loose before taking his last agonizing breath…

Chapter 1

November 1942

"Looks like those Limeys and their tough bastard of a general, Montgomery, have ol' Rommel on the run in North Africa," Packy Farmer of the *Herald American* proclaimed approvingly between drags on his gnarled little hand-rolled cigarette as he scanned the front page of the *Sun*. "Could just be the beginning of the end for the goddamn Jerries."

Anson Masters huffed and passed a hand over his freckled bald pate, possibly hoping to locate a surviving hair. "Sad to say that's wishful thinking, Cyril," the dean of the Police Headquarters press corps countered, using the given name Farmer detested. "We're in this mess for years and years. Don't count on the Germans and their *wehrmacht* to go away anytime soon."

"Oh, hell, what do you know about it, Antsy?" Farmer shot back. "You've never been closer to warfare than the time you ducked behind a squad car on South Wabash, when that whorehouse got raided and some second-rate hoodlum panicked, ran out the front door, and started shooting at anything that moved. But he missed you, as I recall."

5

"Hey, don't go making sport of our fine Mister Masters," Dirk O'Farrell of the *Sun* cut in somberly. "The old gentleman here was just doing his job–covering the news of this great metropolis–and I salute him for the effort." The amazing thing was that he spoke those words without the slightest trace of sarcasm, indicating that O'Farrell had a promising future as a dramatic actor or a politician.

At this point, allow me to step forward and set the stage. The individuals who have been speaking, along with myself and one Eddie Metz of the *Times* (you'll meet him soon enough, but don't hold your breath–he's not worth it), comprise the press corps, as in reporters, at Police Headquarters, 1121 S. State St., Chicago. We all have been here, representing our respective newspapers, for more years than each of us cares to admit, although in O'Farrell's case, he's on his second Chicago paper. The lanky, white-haired journeyman, who's about the same age as Masters–roughly their early sixties–was with Hearst's *Herald and Examiner* until it merged with the *American* in '39 to form the *Herald American*, if you're still with me.

Farmer, with his thin mustache and black hair parted in the center and slicked down with brilliantine, looked like Hollywood central casting's version of a riverboat gambler. Before coming to Chicago in the early '30s, he had worked on papers across the country, leaving a trail of bad checks, angry women, and vengeful husbands.

6

After the Hearst papers' merger, he landed the *Herald American's* job at Police Headquarters, while O'Farrell became odd man out, or one too many here. Dirk got stuck on rewrite for said *Herald American* and wasn't happy about it: When Marshall Field started his *Chicago Sun* three days before Pearl Harbor in December of '41, Dirk was in their offices like a lightning bolt, and he got his old Headquarters beat back, albeit with a brand-new daily.

Me, I'm with the *Tribune*, one of the five big papers in this town, and with the largest circulation by far. And, as I realize from looking at the words above, you don't know that Anson Masters' employer is the *Daily News*, the second-best paper in the city next to the *Trib* or the best, depending on your perspective.

There is one other desk in the dismal press room with its dirty, peeling, pea-green walls, and grimy windows facing the elevated tracks. It belongs to the City News Bureau of Chicago, more commonly known as City Press, a local news service that feeds police, government, and courtroom news to all of the daily papers as well as the radio stations. It serves as a journalism training ground in that its woefully paid reporters are usually young, many fresh from college and in some cases even from high school, and they get rotated from beat to beat around town. Many later end up on daily papers, as I myself did.

One change wrought by this war is that City Press began hiring young women to fill the ranks depleted by enlistments and the draft. One of them, a young redhead named Joanie, just out of the journalism school at Northwestern, was at least for now a member of our press room crew, ending its all-male composition. She seemed very bright and eager to learn, and her presence has had the effect of cleaning up our language to some degree.

It was a typical morning in the Headquarters press room–coffee, cigarettes, and spirited badinage, all suggestive of work avoidance. We each had reached the stage where we were essentially putting in our time, although as the best writer by far in this crew, I still had aspirations.

"Hey Snap, anything new on your request?" O'Farrell asked as he leaned back, feet on his desk. He was referring to my ongoing appeals to *Trib* management to be made a war correspondent.

"Of course not," I grumped. "Again last week, the assistant managing editor gave me the old litany: Cromie, Noderer, Gallagher, Korman, Thompson, and so on."

"Well, you do have to admit that's a pretty damn strong lineup," Farmer put in. "Especially Bob Cromie dodging Jap bullets at Guadalcanal and that wild man Thompson jumping out of airplanes, for God's sake." He was referring to Jack Thompson, a *Trib* reporter assigned to North Africa, who had parachuted with the U.S. troops, a first for a foreign correspondent.

"A bit of showboating, if you ask me," Anson Masters proclaimed. "Anything for a headline." Masters'

8

Daily News was the only other local paper with a major investment in war correspondents, so if you choose to read envy into his comment, be my guest.

"Shame you can't enlist, Snap," O'Farrell said with genuine sympathy. "You're getting up there, but you're still of an age where they could take you if you hadn't..."

"If I hadn't had rheumatic fever on my medical records," I said, completing Dirk's sentence. "Even though that was back when I was thirteen."

"Hell, Malek, you can't go blaming the good ol' U.S. Army. They wouldn't want you croaking of a heart attack in the middle of a battle, would they?" Eddie Metz wheezed between puffs on a Spud, one of the low-grade wartime menthol smokes. Eddie, all five-feet-four of him, if you include the unkempt mass of hair crowning his flat head like a floor mop, was usually the last one to jump into any press room discussion, and as usual he had the least to contribute.

"No, Eddie, the country certainly wouldn't want me croaking on the battlefield," I said to him in a world-weary voice. "Heaven forbid I might die from something other than a gunshot wound or a hand grenade."

O'Farrell leaned forward, palms down on his desk. "Now, back in the first war–"

"Aw, come on, Dirk," Packy Farmer cut in, "not the same old stories about your so-called exploits as a doughboy with Black Jack Pershing's American Expeditionary Force in France in '18. We've heard all we

9

want to about your bravery under fire, although we have yet to see a medal."

O'Farrell shrugged and threw his hands up. "All right, since you boys don't choose to learn from history, I'll just keep my valued war experiences to myself. You all will be the poorer for it."

"We will try to live with that deprivation, Dirk," Anson Masters said dryly. "May I suggest that it's time we get to work and earn our keep?" As the senior member of the press room, he invariably called a halt to our morning bull sessions and signaled the true start of the work day. For me, the least-lazy member of the Headquarters crew, that meant my daily trip to the office of the Chief of Detectives, Fergus Sean Fahey, very likely the savviest man on the force.

I had drawn the Detective Bureau years before. It is by far the best beat in the old building, and when I got transferred–or demoted–to Headquarters after problems with the bottle that cost me my marriage and very nearly my job, my fellow press room habitués strongly suggested I take on the homicide beat. The reason they gave was that because homicide generates the most news and the *Tribune* has the biggest news hole by far of any paper in town, I was the logical choice. The reality, however, was that none of them wanted a beat that entailed real work. As we all shared each other's information anyway, making a joke of the phrase "competitive journalism," whatever news I got from Fahey and his crew would become theirs as well.

As for my drinking, I've never totally quit, but I now limit myself to beer, and only a modest amount of that. Most of the time anyway.

I sauntered into Fahey's small anteroom and was greeted by the smiling and easy-on-the-eyes face of one Elsie Dugo. She had been guarding the chief's door almost as long as I had been making frontal attacks on it.

"Well, if it isn't Steven 'Snap' Malek, intrepid boy reporter and man about town," she said, batting her eyelashes with exaggerated coquetry.

"Aw shucks now, little lady, ah just came ridin' into town this very mornin' and thought ah might get a few minutes with your local U.S. marshal."

"Well, cowpoke, shake the trail dust off your chaps and I'll see if our local marshal is available." She spoke into the intercom and got a crackling reply that sounded vaguely like "send him in."

Fergus Fahey, stocky, gray of hair, and ruddy of face, sat behind his battered brown desk, shuffling papers. He didn't look up as I eased myself into one of his two ancient and unmatched guest chairs.

"Good morning, sir, so nice to see you again," I said, tossing my pack of Lucky Strikes onto his blotter. "Just remember, now that it's white instead of green, we're helping the war effort." I was referring to the fact that Luckies had recently switched their package color from green to white because they said green dye was needed

11

for the war effort.

"You really believe that hooey?" Fahey asked as he pulled out a cigarette and fired it up.

"Nah, but it makes for a good radio commercial with that tag line, 'Lucky Strike green has gone to war.' And you can't beat the publicity."

"I suppose," the chief said absently. "And I also suppose you want some of Elsie's coffee."

"You suppose right. As you know, it's rumored to be the best in the building."

"That's no rumor," he said, hitting his intercom button three times, the coffee signal. Within seconds, Elsie came in and set a steaming mug of her brew on the desk. I blew her a kiss and got one in return.

Fahey leaned back and interlaced his hands behind his head. "Now, what can I do for you, Snap? Or did you just come for the coffee and to ogle Elsie, as I suspect is usually the case?"

I tried to look hurt. "Fergus, how can you say that? You know I am drawn to this office every day because of your warmth, your engaging personality, and of course your sense of humor."

"Right. Which is why Fred Allen and Jack Benny are probably shaking in their boots for fear that I'll get a comedy show opposite one of them on another network. Now that we have that out of the way, there must be some case you want to ask about." It was clear Fergus wanted to get rid of me, and go back to his stack of paperwork.

"Not really. I thought maybe you had something for me and for the hundreds of thousands of readers out there who love nothing more than a good juicy murder."

Fahey stubbed out what was left of his cigarette and reached into my pack for another. "Things are awfully quiet at the moment–not that I'm complaining, mind you. But there is something…"

"Yeah?"

"Well, it's not really in my bailiwick, but at the commissioner's weekly meeting, where all of the department heads and the precinct commanders get together, Grady–you know him, the lieutenant who runs the Hyde Park station–feels like something's going on down there, but he can't seem to get a handle on it. Anybody on your paper heard any rumblings?"

"Not that I know of, but I'll nose around. Let me get this straight: *you're* asking *me* for information? Now there's a switcheroo."

"Why not, given all the stuff I've fed you over the years?" the chief snapped. "And if you didn't have that story-sharing crap in the press room, you'd have had a pile of exclusives for your paper."

I grinned. "Point taken. Hyde Park's usually pretty peaceful, isn't it? Low crime statistics and all?"

"Sure. And why not? It's mainly filled with quiet old houses and those nice, sedate apartment buildings and hotels along South Shore Drive, plus the University–and thanks to that intellectual snob president of theirs,

Hutchins, they don't even play football anymore, so the Saturdays are quiet. Plus there's that Rosenwald Museum in Jackson Park–or I guess we're officially calling it the Museum of Science & Industry now, right?"

"A Rosenwald by any other name," I deadpanned, waiting for Fahey, a rare cop who reads Shakespeare, to react. He did.

"One more remark like that and I'll have Elsie revoke your coffee privileges," he muttered, cupping a hand to his mouth to hide a grin.

"You do and it's no more Luckies," I countered. "But back to the subject: Exactly what makes Grady uneasy about Hyde Park?"

Fahey furrowed his ruddy brow. "He wasn't very specific. But apparently little old ladies in those big houses north of the Midway, along streets like Kenwood and Dorchester, have claimed to see a lot of new faces along their sidewalks. Not students, they insist, but older people, men. Some of them look 'foreign,' they say, whatever that's supposed to mean." Fahey paused to take a drag on his cigarette. "These dowagers spend a lot of time watching the world from their parlors, and they're not shy about calling the police with every little thing, from boys throwing stones at stray dogs to the occasional drunk relieving himself under a streetlight at night."

"Maybe those ladies haven't changed much over the years, but they're the exception," I said. "The war has altered things almost everywhere else. For instance, the

14

other day we had a photo in the *Trib* of sailors drilling right there on the Midway. You wouldn't have seen that before Pearl Harbor."

"Yeah, you're right," Fahey agreed. "Things are different damn near everywhere now. And to be honest– not for the record, of course–Grady tends to be something of a fussbudget, overreacting to residents' complaints. I was actually a little embarrassed for him at the meeting. When he came out with his comment, there were some looks exchanged between precinct commanders."

"Well, as I said, I'll do some nosing around anyway."

"Hardly high priority," Fahey muttered dismissively. "It's probably nothing."

"Probably," I agreed, rising. "Keep the pack of Luckies."

"My lucky day," Fahey said with a poker face, undoubtedly expecting a groan from me. He got it.

Chapter 2

I'd like to report that I followed up quickly on Fergus Fahey's request about Hyde Park, but when I got back to the press room, Dirk O'Farrell was beginning to brief the others about a hot item he picked up from the Vice Squad, one of his beats.

"...so yesterday they broke up this high-priced call girl ring, and is it a doozie," he said, savoring the limelight. "Seems that these, er...*ladies* operated out of an apartment on North Lake Shore Drive, up around Belmont Harbor. And their clientele–listen to this." Dirk then proceeded to read off a list of names. It included two top trial lawyers, one divorce lawyer, a senior vice president at one of the city's biggest banks, a well-known radio personality, a Cubs pitcher, a society band leader, a North Side Protestant minister, and three men I would term "socialites," given that their pictures are on the society pages every week.

"Now I call *that* an all-star lineup," Eddie Metz said approvingly, smacking his lips and slurping coffee.

"Indeed it is," Anson Masters intoned. "But other than general details, the name of the madam and some

17

quotes from the puffed-up commander of the Vice Squad, where does that put us? My editors certainly will not print the names of these now-tarnished luminaries, names which of course our readers crave. And in point of fact, one of the lawyers on that roster–I'm not at liberty to say which–plays golf regularly with my managing editor at an exclusive North Shore country club."

"How 'bout you, Eddie?" Packy Farmer said with a smirk. "As the only tabloid we've got in this town, your rag will print just about anything, right?"

Metz looked uncomfortable. "Uh…I don't think I could get these names past my brother and onto the page," he muttered. Tom "Hotshot" Metz was the bombastic city editor of the *Times*, surely the sole reason Eddie had a job on the paper.

"Well, well," Masters said, looking around the room. "It would appear that no one of us will print the names. What about our young lady from City News?" He dipped his chin in Joanie's direction.

She colored slightly. "I don't think so," she replied softly. "None of you would print them anyway, and I don't believe any of the radio stations would choose to use them either, do you?"

"Certainly not the station whose guy got caught with his trousers down around his ankles," O'Farrell guffawed, swiveling toward the City News desk. "I bet they didn't prepare you for this in the hallowed halls up at good old Northwestern now, did they, Joan?"

"Not really. They never taught us how to write whorehouse stories in Crime Reporting 101," she deadpanned, eliciting a round of laughter. Even though she got a good deal of teasing in the press room, we'd all come to like Joan in the weeks she'd been with us, to the extent of taking a somewhat paternal interest in her. And she was learning to give as well as she got in the office banter.

Even without names, the call-girl story got big play in the afternoon editions of the *Daily News, Herald American*, and *Times*, as well as in the next morning's *Trib* and *Sun*, with banner heads in all five papers and photos of both the Vice Squad Commander and the Police Commissioner. It even bumped the war news down to second position on every front page, if only for one day.

But all the papers did list the lines of work of the men whose names were listed in the madam's little black book, although the Cubs pitcher simply became "a major league baseball player" in print. It wasn't hard to imagine all the speculation going on around town as to the identities of these customers, and it undoubtedly led to guessing games at water coolers and poker games and cocktail parties over the next several weeks.

I got pumped myself by the regulars at Kilkenny's, the saloon on North Clark Street near my apartment that was my favorite hangout. But I chose to play dumb.

"Aw, come on, Snap," Morty Easterly pleaded from his semi-permanent stool at the far end of the bar. "You musta learned who they were from the cops."

"Nope, sorry, Morty," I lied, "they only gave us their professions. Your guesses are as good as mine."

He and the others kept after me, even throwing out names as possibilities, but they tired of getting no response from me after a couple of nights of badgering, so the subject died down, both in Kilkenny's and in the newspapers as well.

For us local reporters, though, it had been fun to grab some headlines, if only briefly, from the war correspondents in Europe, Africa, and the Pacific. Only after the call-girl story had run its course did I remember Fahey's query about Hyde Park. It was an area I had covered on occasion in my early days as a City News Bureau reporter, although that was well over a decade ago.

The few times I could recall being in Hyde Park for reasons other than work was when I ushered at football games at Stagg Field back in my high school days. We didn't get paid, but we got to see the games, back when the Maroons, as they were called, were a football powerhouse. That was long before the school's administration decided it wasn't interested in being up there with the big boys, schools like Michigan and Notre Dame and Southern Cal.

I started by phoning MacAfee, the *Trib* reporter on the South Police beat, which meant he covered all of the precinct stations in roughly the southern third of the city.

"Hello, Mr. Malek," he said in a polite tone when I'd gotten hold of him at the Hyde Park precinct station. Al MacAfee was one of the paper's youngest reporters, earnest, hard-working, and eager to please.

"Just wondering, Mac, if you've heard about anything unusual going on in Hyde Park. I'm checking out a tip from an informant."

"Hmm, interesting to hear that. Seems that Grady, the precinct commander, is concerned as well. Says that he's gotten reports about so-called strangers prowling the neighborhoods around the university. But I tend to discount a lot of what he says–he's a good cop but something of a worry-wart. Did your tipster have any specifics?"

"Not really. Pretty much the same thing Grady said. More strangers around than usual, some of them maybe foreign."

MacAfee exhaled. "Well, from what I've seen of the university, a lot of the professors look pretty strange themselves. And a lot of them are probably foreign, too. But other than that, I don't know of anything out of the ordinary. Actually, it's a pretty quiet area most of the time. Oh, you've got the occasional drunken campus party, of course. And there are house burglaries from time to time, but it's usually pretty routine stuff. Very few murders. Other sections of town have lots more crime, as I'm sure you know."

I told him thanks, signed off, and thumbed my dog-eared address book for the number of one Charlie "Pickles" Podgorny, a small-time grifter and the only person I knew well who lived out south, although he was in Englewood, not Hyde Park.

Pickles owed me a favor. Back in '39, the cops hauled him in for running a crap game just two blocks from Police Headquarters in the back room of a saloon over on Wabash. I was impressed with his balls for gambling in the very shadow of the law, and I went to his hearing to see what kind of guy would pull such a stunt. I liked him instantly–short, squat, swarthy, bow-legged, and with a collection of colorful stories about con men, gamblers, and the shadowy world of the city's nocturnal underbelly that would have endeared him to Damon Runyon. While I was interviewing him for a possible feature (which never ran), he asked me for help, and I hooked him up with a lawyer I knew who got him off with a modest fine and a judge's Biblical admonition to "go, and sin no more."

As far as I know, Pickles may have continued to sin in any number of ways, but apparently he hadn't got caught at it. And because of his gratitude to me, I on several occasions asked him to do some legwork for me on stories. He seemed to know every two-bit bookie, hustler, fence, and small-time gambler south of Roosevelt Road, and at least twice he steered me toward a source that helped me flesh out a piece, particularly a Sunday feature on some aspect of crime.

Surprisingly, I reached him right away. "Pickles—what are you doing at home in the afternoon? Resting up for some action with those little six-sided cubes that have dots on them?"

"Snap, old compadre—nice to hear your voice, my good man! But surely you jest. I've put my evil days behind me, and now I content myself with an occasional game of pasteboards with some friends right here in the neighborhood."

"Uh-huh. Perhaps as in five-card stud with table stakes?"

"Perhaps," he chuckled. "And sometimes even seven-card stud. But it's just a friendly game, call it a pastime."

"Right. And a pastime which usually finds you with a fatter wallet at the end than at the start."

"Oh, from time to time I am able to depart the table with what might be described as some modest earnings. Of course, the real joy for me is the companionship of kindred souls, not the transfer of legal tender. But Snap, as dear a friend as I know you to be, I sense that you haven't called simply to inquire as to my recreational activities."

"You sense correctly, old timer. I hear rumors about something going on in Hyde Park, and it occurred to me that you, too, might have heard rumblings."

"Cannot say as I have, Snap. As you know, it's a quiet community, extremely intellectual, of course. How

23

specific are these rumors you hear?"

"Not very–just that something seems to be in the air. Could be the result of hyperactive imaginations."

"Tell you what, newshound. I'll go up there and poke around. Shoot, that neighborhood is almost next door to me anyway, and I know a hangout on 55th Street called the "U.T."–stands for University Tavern. Students, locals, all sorts hang out in there. It's a lively spot, serves food as well as drink. I've been there a few times for a refreshing libation, and I might just pick something up. Nothing like a public house to learn what's going on in the environs. But I don't suppose you'd know that, would you?"

"Don't be too sure of that, Pickles. I, too, sometimes go out in search of a refreshing libation. And by the way, I will reimburse you for any of the liquids that you might happen to consume at this Hyde Park watering hole."

"Words I was hoping to hear. We shall stay in touch."

Chapter 3

With American entry into the war now nearing the one-year mark, increasing numbers of us were impacted. Consider the Headquarters press room alone:

Although I could not enlist because of my history of rheumatic fever, I did have a cousin who was serving. Charlie Malek, son of my late father's younger brother Frank, was a corporal with an Army unit that had just landed in Algeria. I checked every week or so with Uncle Frank and Aunt Edna to see how he was faring. He wrote them almost daily, and Frank would sometimes read portions of a letter to me over the phone, including one in which Charlie wrote that his closest buddy in the platoon had been killed instantly by a mortar blast not twenty yards from him.

Anson Masters' grandson served on a destroyer in the Pacific and from the deck had witnessed the sinking of the aircraft carrier *USS Yorktown* at the Battle of Midway.

Dirk O'Farrell's stepson Dean served as a navigator on a B24 Liberator bomber that had just begun flying missions over Germany from an airbase in Britain. Dirk came into the press room one morning and reported that

Dean's plane had been hit by anti-aircraft fire and limped back across the English Channel on two engines and a disabled landing gear. "They made a bumpy landing," Dirk told us, "but everybody survived, although Dean got a concussion and the nose gunner suffered three broken ribs and a busted leg."

Scott, the older brother of Joanie from City News, was less fortunate. He was an Army lieutenant stationed at Bataan in the Philippines when the Japanese overran the peninsula in April, and he was one of thousands of U.S. troops captured by the Japanese. He has not been heard from in months and either was captured or is dead, most likely a casualty of the infamous "Bataan Death March." We have stopped asking Joanie about him, hoping (but doubtful) that one morning she will come in with happy news.

I still hadn't heard from Pickles Podgorny a couple of mornings later when, in the Headquarters press room, I opened my three-star final edition of the *Trib*. "I'll be damned," I said to no one in particular as I scanned Page 1. "They found Rickenbacker alive at sea, along with those other guys from that plane crash. Only one of 'em died. More than three weeks in rubber life rafts out in the Pacific. What a story."

"Yeah, and here's the corker," Packy Farmer responded, looking over the top of his own copy of the same edition. "A sea gull lands on Rickenbacker's head,

26

he grabs it, and that poor bird becomes a meal for these guys."

"Rick must have nine lives," Eddie Metz marveled, "after everything that happened back in 1918."

"I guess I don't understand," Joanie from City News volunteered.

"No reason you should," Anson Masters responded in his best Dutch-uncle tone. "You're far too young. Along with Sergeant York, Rickenbacker was the gold-plated American hero in what some of us still refer to as the Great War. He was a fearless fighter pilot, a wild man in the skies. He shot down more than twenty German planes in a very short time–a few weeks, I think, back in '18.

"Then along comes this war, and our government, actually Secretary of War Stimson, sends him to the Pacific to look over our air operations there, and his plane goes down in the drink off some God-forsaken place like New Guinea. Ran out of fuel."

"I read about that crash when it happened a few weeks ago, but I didn't read up on his background at the time," she said somberly.

"It's certainly no exaggeration to call the guy a legend," Dirk O'Farrell said between drags on his cigarette. "What we need now is more like him, the way we're struggling. Think there are some new Eddie Rickenbackers around, this time to shoot down the Japanese Zeros and the Nazi Messerschmidts?"

Before anyone could respond, Anson Masters

proclaimed the beginning of the work day. The crew all rose, none with enthusiasm, and filed out the press room door to their various beats. I was just getting up to follow them when my phone rang.

"Hey, Snap, got a minute?" It was Pickles.

"For you, I always have a minute," I said as the last of the press corps left the room. "What, pray tell, have you learned?"

"I hadn't been on the campus in a good long time, and things have really changed, Snap," he said. "Whole buildings have been boarded up, and they're off limits. They've got uniformed guards, soldiers that is, keeping people out. In fact, there are uniforms all over the school, and by that I don't mean cops."

"Army?"

"Army, Navy, the works. Place looks like a damn military base."

"Not so surprising," I said. "I've been reading that colleges across the country are filling up with military recruits taking courses that will help them get a commission–something called V-12, although I don't know what it means."

"Well, these guys are all over the place–even in the bars. Although not in uniform then."

"Which I'm sure you quickly discovered, Pickles."

"Hey, I did tell you I was going to visit the U.T. at 55th and University, which I did."

"Okay, and what came of that visit, other than the

consumption of some amber-colored liquid?"

Pickles cleared his throat. "The place was mobbed–students, maybe some faculty members if I was to guess their professions, a few blue-collar-type guys who look like they might drive trucks or work in the stockyards, and also a number of soldiers and sailors, at least that's what I think; they were wearing civilian clothes. I was lucky to find a stool at the bar, so I plopped myself down and ordered a stein of draught. And a very good draught it was."

"Pickles, I'm happy to learn that you were able to please your palate, at my expense, I might add. But is this narrative going anywhere?"

"I'm getting to it, my typewriter jockey friend. After I'd been in the place…oh, maybe half an hour or so, a couple of joes with tweed sports jackets and ties, they were maybe in their late thirties or so, coulda been profs maybe, sit down just to my right, and they're talking about the war, see?"

"A natural subject these days."

"Yeah, well the one guy, he's all mopey about how our boys are takin' a pounding both in Europe and out in the Pacific. He's really depressed, says he'll probably get drafted just in time to see the Jerries invade New York and the Japs take over San Francisco."

"A real cheerful Charlie, eh?"

"Uh-huh. But what the other guy, who has a little beard, says then really gets me to listening close."

"Which was?"

"He says, 'If you only knew what I know, you wouldn't have any worries at all about us winning this war.' The other guy asks him what he means by that, and the bearded one starts to clam up."

"So that's all?"

"Will you let me tell it, Snap? The mopey guy keeps on pushing, and the other one starts getting kinda nervous and doesn't want to say any more. They lower their voices, see, but even with all the noise in that saloon, I got real good ears. Comes from listening for footsteps from outside when I'm in the middle of a crap game. Or *used to be* in the middle of a game."

"So stipulated. Pray continue, before I have to break for lunch."

"Very funny. Anyway, the mopey one, he keeps askin' questions, and the beard says something big is goin' on right there on the campus, so big it's gonna change the whole world, he says.

"The mope then asks if that's why some of the school's buildings are boarded up and off limits now with soldiers out in front, and the other guy nods his head, but he won't say any more."

"Interesting. Did you get the impression this man of secrets hangs out in that saloon regularly?"

"Couldn't tell for sure, Snap. Although he did seem like he knew the barkeep, a fellow named Chester."

"Good sign. Can I talk you into being in that same

saloon again this evening, Pickles? I'll pick up the tab, as well as reimburse you for last night, of course."

"I had planned on taking a chair in a friendly little game of five-card draw with some friends in my neighborhood, but they're always there for the plucking, so I will graciously accept your generosity. What time?"

"When did you see this fellow last night?"

"A little after eight."

"I'll be in the U.T. at eight tonight."

Leaving work at twenty past five–the *Trib's* evening man, Ellis, was invariably late in relieving me–I decided to hang around downtown instead of going north to my apartment on Clark Street near Wrigley Field. I polished off a so-so beef potpie and not-very-good coffee in a little beanery on Van Buren, under the elevated tracks just west of State, and then made up for it with two steins of very good beer in the grand old Berghoff Restaurant on Adams. Thus fortified, I took the Illinois Central electric train down to the university community of Hyde Park, no more than fifteen minutes south of the Loop.

Being late fall, it was of course long past sundown when I got off the train at 55th Street and went down the dank concrete stairway to the street. The evening was mild, which made my stroll through the little business district around the station a pleasant one. The neighborhood was quiet, at least outside the University Tavern...the din hit me the moment I opened the door to

31

the watering hole, which seemed to be filled with the entire population of Hyde Park, every one of them yakking and drinking and smoking.

Through the nicotine-blue haze, I spotted Pickles Podgorny on a stool about halfway along a bar at which every seat was taken. He gave me a salute and ambled over.

"Got here early, mate," he said, cupping a hand to my ear to be heard above the clamor. "Wanted to make sure I got a spot next to the guy. That's him." He gestured to a dark-haired, bearded specimen hunched over the seat beside the one he had just vacated, although the half-filled stein on the bar indicated the stool still had an occupant.

I thanked Pickles, let him take his beer away, and sat down, looking straight ahead. After about a half minute, the bartender came over and I ordered a Blue Ribbon on draught. "Things don't look so good for our boys these days overseas, do they?" I asked when he delivered the frosted stein.

The barkeep, a burly, bull-necked specimen of about forty-five, who was indeed named Chester, shrugged. "I dunno, seems to me like we're doing better in the Pacific these days. Y'know, Coral Sea, Midway, those navy battles, they turned out okay."

I shrugged, avoiding any glance at the figure on my right. "At least that's what we're being told," I said. "But even at Midway, for Pete's sake, we lost that carrier, the *Yorktown*. And after all the ships that got sent to the

32

bottom at Pearl Harbor, we sure as hell can't afford to keep losing them. I still say these are bad times."

My pessimism finally drew a reaction from the right, as I had intended. "Things are going to get better, a lot better, you can bank on that," the bearded fellow said to me, spacing his last five words for emphasis.

"Really? You think so?" I swiveled to face him. He looked to be in his late thirties, as Pickles had estimated, with shaggy dark hair hanging down to the tops of equally shaggy eyebrows and a beard that hadn't seen a trimming in weeks, maybe months. Thick-lensed horned-rim glasses magnified coal-black eyes, giving him a manic appearance.

"I *know* so," he stated, as if daring contradiction.

I watched him as I sipped my beer. "You seem awfully confident. I wish I could be."

He allowed himself a slight smile. "You don't know what I know," he said smugly.

"Sounds like we've got some kind of a secret weapon," I replied, intent on keeping the conversation alive.

Another brief smile. "At the place where we surrendered...that's where we shall rise again," he announced, setting his stein down firmly on the bar as if to add an exclamation point to his cryptic comment. "A good evening to you, sir—and to you as well, Chester," he said, nodding and rising to leave.

"Unusual fellow," I remarked to the bartender.

33

"That's the professor," Chester said as he wiped the polished mahogany surface of the bar. "Comes in here a lot."

"He certainly seems confident about the war," I said as Pickles Podgorny slid into the just-vacated seat beside me.

"Sure, and I am too," the man behind the bar said with a touch of belligerence in his voice. "What's the matter, aren't you patriotic?"

"I am indeed. But that doesn't keep me from worrying. That professor talks like he seems to know something."

Chester turned his beefy palms up. "He knows a lot about a lot of stuff, but then he's a wisehead. They's different from you and me."

"I won't argue that point. What does he teach?"

"Beats me, I wouldn't understand it anyway. Something about physics, I think. Over there." He made a head gesture in the general direction of the campus.

"Thanks," I told him, getting up. "What did you say his name is?"

"I didn't, but it's Bergman."

It was a name I was not to forget.

Chapter 4

In the half-dozen years since my divorce, my weekend routine had been essentially regimented. On Saturday mornings, I would pick up my son Peter at the apartment on North Lake Shore Drive where he lived with Norma and her husband, Martin Baer. We would then spend Saturday and most of Sunday together, and I would drop him off at the Baer household Sunday evening.

As Peter had gotten older–he was now a sophomore at Lake View High–it had gotten more difficult for me to find activities we could do together. He felt he'd pretty well outgrown the Riverview amusement park, and over the years we had seen most of the museums in town several times. There were still Cubs games in the summer, and movies. We both liked westerns and war films.

Peter often had enough homework that he had to spend time with his books while he was at my place. Most important to me was that even as he had gotten older, he still wanted to spend time with his dad, although I knew this would soon change. His growing consciousness of his female classmates meant that

Saturday nights soon would be reserved for something other than hanging out with the old man.

In the last year, he also had become interested in football and, even with his slight frame, he had made the Lake View junior varsity squad as a reserve. This interest in the game now extended to the Chicago Bears. He had never seen them play, and a couple of times had asked me if it was hard to get tickets. It was damned hard, particularly as the Bears had won the league championship the last two years and looked like they were going to do it again with another powerhouse squad.

The *Trib's* sports staff was notoriously stingy in sharing passes to games–in any sport–with members of other departments. On a couple of occasions previously, I had pressed Leo Cahill, a copyreader on the sports copy desk, for Bears tickets for me and Peter, and each time he'd told me there weren't any. "Geez, Snap, I'd love to help you out, but these ducats are scarcer than hen's teeth. I'm lucky if I get to one game a year myself."

Now Leo and I are not what you would call close friends, never have been. He's a devout Catholic, or so he likes to inform me regularly, and on several occasions he has pointed out, none too subtly, my lapsed status as a member of the Church of Rome. Also, Leo is that relative rarity, a teetotaling Irishman, and he has delighted in mentioning what he refers to as my "Achilles heel"– specifically, my periodic tendency to overindulge, a tendency I have for the most part overcome these last few years. But to the sanctimonious Leo, I shall forever be one of the fallen, as both a worshiper and an imbiber.

Right now, however, I needed Leo Cahill, and I saw a way to get what I wanted.

"Are you behaving yourself?" I asked as I phoned him from my desk in the Police Headquarters press room on a Friday afternoon.

"Snap Malek, what brings a call from you?" he asked with a forced bonhomie. "Need beer money?"

"No, Mr. Cahill," I said, gritting my teeth, "I would never impose on you in that way, especially knowing your strong feelings about the evils of demon rum. What I am interested in is two tickets to Sunday's Bears-Packers game." Leo let loose with a guffaw that must have startled his co-workers on the sports copy desk. "Oh, Snap, you know that's a hot ticket right now, and impossible to get. Sorry old pal."

"Well, just thought I'd ask. By the way, Leo, how's your Knights of Columbus fund drive going, the one to make sure kids on the South Side have Christmas presents this year?"

I was met with silence at the other end for perhaps ten seconds. "We can always use some help," Leo said in a suddenly subdued tone. I knew from an article in one of the papers that the K of C campaign for kids was struggling.

"Hmm. Well, I've got a double sawbuck that I would be happy to pony up if…well, if someone saw fit to, shall we say, give something in return."

"Snap, that's playing dirty," Leo responded in a hushed tone; it sounded like he was cupping the speaker with his hand.

"Leo, I never play dirty, you should know that as an old friend. I'm hurt that you would suggest such a thing."

Silence from the other end, followed by a drawn-out sigh. "Twenty dollars, you say?"

"Coin of the realm, Leo, coin of the realm. In exchange for two tickets, Bears-Packers, close to the fifty-yard line."

"Now come on, Snap," he whined. "That's unreasonable."

"I'm holding the double sawbuck in my hand, Leo, and Andrew Jackson is looking back at me sternly. This piece of paper could buy two or three, or maybe four nice gifts for some needy kids. I might even be persuaded to add an Abe Lincoln–that's a fin, for your information. You can do a lot with twenty-five simoleons these days."

Another silence on the line, followed by another sigh. "Do they have to be on the fifty-yard line?"

"No, Leo, I said close to the fifty. But we want to at least be between the forty-yard lines. Don't try to tell me our fine Sports Department can't come up with something in that vicinity."

He didn't bother to sigh this time. "Okay…that's twenty-five bucks, right?"

"Twenty-five for a great cause, Leo."

"All right. I'll have the tickets in an envelope here with your name on it."

"And I'll leave an envelope with your name on it, and the greenbacks inside. You're a truly fine gentleman, Leo."

"Yeah," he muttered.

When I picked Peter up on Lake Shore Drive Saturday morning, I was pleased to tell Norma and Martin Baer that we had tickets to the game. Baer, who I had to concede was a decent fellow, could provide for Norma and Peter in ways I couldn't have begun to match. His men's haberdashery over in the Lincoln-Belmont-Ashland area apparently turned a dandy profit, because he owned an eight-room co-op on the twelfth floor overlooking the lake and took his wife and stepson to Florida every winter. So going to a Bears-Packers game with my son was at least a small victory, almost equal to my getting us seats four years earlier for a Cubs-Yankees World Series game. Peter still talked about that afternoon, and about meeting Dizzy Dean in the locker room after the game.

And so it was that on a Sunday afternoon, remarkably mild and more typical of late September than mid-November, Peter and I left my third-floor apartment on North Clark Street, after a lunch of grilled cheese sandwiches and tomato soup, and started on the three-block walk north to Wrigley Field. Before we got halfway there, we began running into American entrepreneurs: "Here's two, thirty-yard line," one beer-breathed guy in a flat cap rasped, thrusting a pair of tickets at us. "Over here, I got four, upper deck, sixth row," a gaunt specimen in a threadbare sport coat brayed, vigorously waving the fanned offerings above his head.

"How come they're selling tickets on the street, Dad?" Peter wanted to know after we had pushed past the fourth hustler.

"They're called scalpers–somehow they get hold of tickets at face value and then sell 'em for inflated prices. It only works when there's a big demand for seats, like today."

"Is it legal?"

"No, but the cops don't usually do anything about it; they've got too much other stuff to worry about." (Chicago's Finest proved me wrong this time: As I was to learn in Monday's paper, they had indeed hauled in several of these independent ticket "merchants.")

Our own seats, true to Leo Cahill's promise, were excellent, about ten rows back on the north forty-five yard line, which in baseball terms put them about halfway between the third-base dugout and the home bullpen. Both teams were still working out as we got settled in, and Peter searched the field for the Bears' premier player, Sid Luckman.

"There he is, number forty-two, just throwing a pass," I told him. "The top quarterback in the league. But you already knew that, didn't you?"

Peter nodded enthusiastically. "And these are the two best teams in football, right?"

"Without a doubt, along with the Washington club. The Redskins are a cinch to win the East title, and we haven't lost a game this year. Green Bay's only been beaten once, by the Bears early in the season. We win today, and we'll be back in the championship game for the third year in a row."

"And what about George Halas, Dad? He's not coaching the Bears anymore, right?"

"He enlisted in the Navy earlier this year. The coach now is Luke Johnsos, he's over there," I said, pointing to a man in a felt hat who was stalking the sidelines and making hand gestures to his players as they warmed up.

Once the game started, it didn't take long for us, along with the other forty-two thousand in the stands, to realize that the Bears would be in the title game again, thanks in large measure to Green Bay's mistakes. In the first quarter, Chicago's center, Bulldog Turner, picked up a Packer fumble and ran 45 yards for a touchdown. Then Luckman, playing on defense as well as offense, intercepted a deflected pass from the Packer quarterback, Isbell, and ran 54 yards to score. The game was all over for the Green Bay boys by halftime, and the Bears went on to a surprisingly easy victory, 38 to 7.

"What a great afternoon," Peter enthused as we left the park. "There's a guy in my class, Charlie Marsh, who moved down from someplace in Wisconsin this year, and

41

he's been telling everybody all week how the Packers were going to really smash the Bears today. I can't wait to see him!"

"Well, go easy on the poor fella," I said. "He'll be feeling none too cheerful tomorrow."

"I can gloat at least a little, though, can't I?"

"Of course, that's what being a fan is all about, especially in a big rivalry. Just remember that some day he may be the one doing the gloating."

"Okay, but I'll worry about that some other time."

"Sounds like a good plan to me," I told him as we walked back to my apartment to celebrate with some ginger ale and chocolate chip cookies.

Chapter 5

Back in the Police Headquarters press room Monday morning, I regaled the crew with a running commentary on the Bears' victory, and I had what seemed to be an enthusiastic audience. In the eleven months since Pearl Harbor, we, along with many other Americans, craved excuses to avoid talking about the war–especially given that our military and naval victories were more than offset by our setbacks. With Chicago's superb pro football team, though, some of us could find an escape, however illusory.

As I reached the point in my narrative where Sid Luckman intercepted a Green Bay pass and dashed for a touchdown, I was interrupted by one Packy Farmer, who had leaned back with his feet on his desk.

"So, oh noble Malek," he intoned between drags on one of his hand-rolled smokes. "You have the power of the mighty, yea omnipotent, *Tribune* behind you so you can spend a Sunday afternoon reveling in the autumnal splendor of the Wrigley coliseum while the rest of us mortals can only dream of seeing first-hand the gladiators from our fair metropolis do pitched battle in said arena

43

against the boys from the north country."

"Oh, button it up, Packy," Dirk O'Farrell snapped. "Let the man finish. You sound like a frustrated sportswriter who's had one too many bottles of Budweiser–and at nine-thirty in the morning, for God's sake!"

"Oh, all right, I yield the floor," Farmer sighed, waving a hand dismissively. "Let the fellow rant on."

"No, no, it's too late," I said, feigning hurt feelings. "The moment is gone; the balloon of excitement has been punctured by the cruel barbs of sarcasm. Just to set the record straight, however, I got those Bears tickets after making a charitable donation."

"That's telling him, Snap," Eddie Metz chortled. "He's just jealous."

"Indeed I am–I don't deny it for a moment," Packy responded. "Would that I were with a paper that has the vast resources of Col. Robert R. McCormick's majestic *Tribune*, which is, as we all know, 'The World's Greatest Newspaper.' We know that because they print those very words on Page 1 every single day."

"Lest we forget them," Anson Masters put in. "I much prefer my own employer's front-page motto, which as you all are aware is: 'An Independent Newspaper.'"

"In this case, 'Independent' equates with wishy-washy," O'Farrell of the *Sun* observed. "If your rag ever took a strong editorial stand on anything, half its readers would pass out from shock."

Masters scowled. "This from a man whose new employer, one Marshall Field III, just started publishing a newspaper late last year. And would anyone present like to remind our Mr. O'Farrell just who prints his newspaper?"

"You do, Antsy," Packy Farmer piped up. "That is, the *Daily News* prints the *Sun* on its presses."

"And why, pray tell, is that?" Masters asked.

"Because Marshall Field doesn't own any presses of his own," Eddie Metz said, enjoying the byplay.

"Just so," Masters responded, looking smug. "Now be nice, Dirk, or we'll evict you from our building over at Madison and Canal. We're doing you a favor by keeping you in business, propping you up as it were."

"Hah–you're doing yourselves a favor," O'Farrell fired back. "Your erstwhile publisher, the eminent Colonel Knox, now FDR's Secretary of the Navy, hates the *Tribune* and its own Colonel–McCormick, that is–so much that he'd do anything to see another morning paper go up against them. Don't pull that 'high-and-mighty' crap on me."

Just as Anson Masters was about to respond, my phone rang and I never heard his retort.

"Hey, Snap, Pickles here."

"What's going on, my poker-playing friend?"

"Probably nothing, but I like to keep you fully informed at all times."

"Of course you do–especially if I'm likely to slip you

45

a few bucks or buy you a few beers."

"Now, Snap, our friendship goes far deeper than money or lager, you know that. Anyway, here's the skinny. The last three nights, I've gone back to that bar in Hyde Park."

"The University Tavern."

"Right. Seems like a convivial place, and I know you were interested in that Bergman chap."

"Go on."

"He hasn't been there three nights running."

"So? Maybe he's got other things to do, like grading papers or some such. After all, it sounds like he's on the faculty down there on the Midway."

"Except I mentioned it to the bartender, Chester, and he was puzzled, too. Said he couldn't remember when the guy had missed even two nights straight. Said he's the most regular customer the U.T. has. Not a heavy imbiber or a troublemaker, just likes to nurse a few beers."

"Your new pal Chester have anything else to add?"

"Just that Bergman, first name Arthur, comes in alone, usually keeps to himself, but occasionally starts chatting with somebody else at the bar, like he did when I first saw him and also when you were there the other night."

"Try going back a couple of more times–that is if it doesn't cramp your other nocturnal pursuits too much. And if Mr. Bergman still hasn't turned up, let me know," I instructed Pickles, figuring that's the last I would hear of this business except for possibly having to slip him a few dollars to cover his beer expenditure. I figured wrong.

Chapter 6

Three days passed before I heard from Pickles again. He rang me late one afternoon in the press room.

"Checking in as ordered, Mr. Newshound. Thought you'd like to know that our Professor Bergman still has not put in an appearance at his favorite watering hole. And Chester, bless his stoic soul, seems more than a little concerned about the absence."

"Has anybody phoned Bergman at home?"

"Ah, I thought you would ask, being the bulldog that you are. The aforesaid Chester says he has called him twice and has received no answer."

"Is our good professor married?"

"Another question that I knew was coming. According to the barkeep, he's been divorced for a year or so, and that one was his second marriage. He lives alone, over on Cornell east of the campus. I looked him up in the phone book," Pickles said proudly.

"You have the makings of a reporter. But Bergman must be showing up for his classes, or the university would have raised some sort of alarm about his absence by now."

49

"Once again, I'm on top of things, Snap. He's not teaching this term. Again, this came from Chester, who's getting suspicious about all the questions I've been asking."

"Pickles, I'm damned if I know why I'm concerned about the whereabouts of one Arthur Bergman, given that I met him just the once and we exchanged only a few words. But he intrigues me–him and that line of his, *'At the place where we surrendered...that's where we shall rise again.'*"

"From what little I saw, he seems confident and not shy about expressing opinions," Pickles said. "But then, professors are supposed to be smart, right?"

"So I've been told. But then, I've had the same amount of college as you–exactly zero."

"Yeah, but the college of hard knocks counts for something, too."

"We'd better hope so. Do you have plans for this evening, Pickles?"

"Nothin' I can't change. What did you have in mind?"

"How about meeting me at the U.T. Say seven-thirty?"

"You've got yourself a deal. I'll be at the bar with a cold draught."

"I'm simply shocked. But since you feel you must imbibe, run a tab–I'll pick it up."

"God bless you, my son," he said with feeling.

* * *

For the second time in a week, I rode the electric train down to Hyde Park with the post-rush hour commuters. True to his word, Pickles sat hunched over the bar with a sweating stein of beer. The saloon was about half-full and half-noisy, and I pulled up a stool next to my trusted South Side informant. He nodded and waved Chester over. "One of these for my friend," he said, nodding in the direction of his beer. The bartender nodded.

"You make it sound like you're treating," I told him. "Damn fine of you."

"Hey, I was just being helpful," he said, trying without success to sound hurt.

"Of course you were. Did you ask Chester again about Bergman?"

"Nah. Like I said on the phone, he already acts like I'm being too nosy about him, so I just came in here tonight and kept my yap shut, other than to order. And he didn't speak to me, other than to say 'Here's your Pabst.'"

"All right–this is the plan: We're going over to Bergman's place on…where is it–Cornell?"

"Yeah, I've got the number. What do you expect to find?" Pickles sounded dubious.

"Probably nothing. He may be holed up in there writing an academic treatise or something like that, which has caused him to break his usual routine. Or he may be too sick to bother answering the phone."

"But wouldn't you think he's got friends who might look in on him?"

"Beats me, maybe they have. But my curiosity is itching and I need to scratch it."

"Okay, scratch away. But then can we come back here for another beer?"

I told him we could, and I paid the check. We left the bar, walking east on 55th Street for several blocks. Passing under the Illinois Central Railroad viaduct, we came to Cornell and turned south.

"It would be this one," Pickles said, consulting the crumpled piece of paper on which he had scribbled the address. He pointed to a three-story U-shaped brick structure with a grassy courtyard that is such a common design for Chicago apartment buildings.

"Snap, what if the guy's at home and answers the door?" Pickles asked. "What do we say then?"

"Well…we can tell him that, uh, the folks at the U.T. were worried about him, and that we volunteered to check on him. How's that?"

"A little lame, considering that neither one of us knows him very well."

"What the hell, Pickles. What's the worst thing that can happen? He'll probably tell us to mind our own business, and that'll be the end of it."

The street door to the small entryway was unlocked. Inside, we found Bergman's name and apartment number, 1-D. I pushed the buzzer above the mailbox and waited.

Nothing. I held it in a second time, longer. Still no response.

I tried the inside door. "It's locked," I said to Pickles.

"Of course it's locked," he said mockingly. "This is Chicago. What did you think? Let me give it a try."

He pulled a ring with at least a dozen keys from his pants pocket and began trying them in the lock without making a sound. On about the third key, the door opened.

We went up the creaky, carpeted stairs the half-flight to 1-D and rapped on the wooden door. Again, no response.

"Now what?" I whispered, mainly to myself.

"Want to get in?" Pickles asked in his own version of a half-whisper.

"As in breaking and entering?"

"Well, you said yourself that the guy may be in there sick or something. He'd thank us."

He pulled out the ring again. This time, it took about five keys before the bolt slid and Pickles eased the door open, again soundlessly.

The stench hit us immediately, reminding me of some other murder scenes where I had been present. I quickly pressed a handkerchief to my mouth and nose. Pickles did likewise.

We sidled into the darkness as I groped for a wall switch. It was where it should have been, and the sudden brightness showed that we were in a drably furnished living room–yellow-striped wallpaper, gray carpet, sofa, three chairs, two floor lamps, one overhead light fixture, two end tables, a floor-model radio, and a desk in one corner covered with papers. The curtains and window shades were drawn.

With Pickles at my heels, I tried to ignore the oppressive malodor and tiptoed across the room to a hallway that led to the rest of the apartment. A tiled bathroom was on the right, empty, a small kitchen on the left with dishes stacked up in the sink, also empty. Straight ahead was the half-open door to what had to be the bedroom.

Associate Professor Arthur Bergman was sprawled on the floor just inside the door, face up. Or rather, what remained of his face, which was eggplant-hued, his mouth frozen open in the death rictus and his coal-black eyes popping out like marbles, staring, unseeing at the ceiling. Sunk deep into his neck was what looked like clothesline, knotted. I retched but stifled the vomit. Pickles retreated to the living room, groaning.

After another cursory look at the body and the room, I joined him. "We're getting out of here right now, you first," I said, still using the near whisper. "Did you touch anything?"

He shook his head vigorously, keeping the hanky pressed against his nose.

"Okay, I'll wipe down the light switch and the doorknobs, now out!" I gave him a not-so-gentle shove toward the door and, using my own handkerchief, turned out the light.

Our luck held. The hall was empty and there was no sound from behind the other apartment door on the landing as we made our way silently down the half-flight of steps to the lobby. Out in the welcome air of a Hyde Park night, we walked rapidly away from the building and did not encounter another pedestrian until we were almost a block down Cornell. Only then did we break the silence.

"Terrible, terrible," Pickles keened. "My God, Snap, how did you know? How did you know?"

"I didn't know. But it seemed awfully strange that the guy had just dropped out of sight. You're sure you didn't touch anything in there?"

"No, God no, I was too busy trying to keep from smelling that…"

"Okay, okay. You've got a record, Pickles. You can't afford to be placed in that apartment, even if the killing happened days ago. With me, it's not as important, although I don't plan to let the law know that I was there."

"You're just going to…leave him?"

"Yes and no," I said, gesturing to a phone booth on the corner under a streetlight. I stepped in, dropped a nickel into the slot, and dialed the police switchboard. When a voice answered, I affected a raspy tone. "I want to report a murder at…I gave the Cornell address…in apartment 1-D." The voice at the other end had begun asking questions as I eased the receiver into its cradle.

"All right, I have fulfilled my duty as a citizen," I told Pickles. "Now I will put on my reporter's hat." I picked up the phone again and dialed the *Tribune* number in the Police Headquarters press room, getting our night man, Ellis, on the second ring.

"Malek here," I told him. "But to you, I'm an anonymous caller. Got that?"

"Yes, sir, Mr. Anonymous Caller, yes sir. And just what can I do for you?"

"It's what I can do for you, Ellis–and for the dear old *Trib*. The police just received a telephone tip that a body had been found in an apartment on South Cornell, not far from the University of Chicago campus. Are you with me so far?"

"Yep, got it down. And I suppose the cops' tip also came from an anonymous caller?"

"That's a good supposition. The dead man is one Arthur Bergman, although the cops likely don't know even that yet. He was apparently on the U of C faculty, probably a physics professor, but I'm not sure. You'll have to check that." I gave Ellis the address and apartment number.

"What else?" he said.

"Mr. Bergman had apparently been strangled with a rope. The body was just inside the bedroom on the floor, fully clothed except for a shirt. He did have his undershirt on, though, which probably means he wasn't expecting anyone. The apartment itself seemed to be pretty much undisturbed, as though there hadn't been a struggle. From a quick look-see, it didn't look like the place had been gone over. All of this is just for your information, of course. The police will probably give out a lot of the same information."

"Sounds suspiciously like you were on the scene. Besides the neck, any other signs of injury?"

"None that were apparent. And by the way, as far as you're concerned, we of course haven't even talked to each other tonight."

"Goes without saying, sir. You anonymous callers must live an interesting after-hours life," Ellis observed dryly.

"Far too interesting on occasion. Have you got everything you need for now?"

"Enough to start making some phone calls around the building."

"Needless to say, I'm curious as to what you learn," I told him, cradling the booth's receiver for a second time.

I stepped out and took two deep breaths. "Now, Pickles, do you still want that second beer?"

"More than ever," he said hoarsely, passing the handkerchief across his forehead. "And a third one, too."

"Sounds good to me. But let's try a different saloon this time. My two visits to the U.T. have been more than enough to last me awhile." Little did I know that I'd be spending a lot more time in the joint in the weeks ahead.

Chapter 7

In fact, Pickles and I put away four more draughts in a small and uncrowded saloon on 53rd Street before we called it a night. I calmed down and stopped shaking before he did, but neither of us had truly unwound until the third stein.

"Geez, Snap, I wasn't expecting to find that. I've seen a few stiffs before, but never one whose face was that color," Pickles said, shaking his head. "What's your take?"

I shrugged and took a long drag on my Lucky. "I don't know. I don't think it was a robbery, because the place didn't look like it had been rifled, although we weren't around long enough to know much."

"Too damn long for my taste. Think it could have been a homo thing?"

"Possible, but I'd say unlikely. The bartender said the guy had been married twice, although that's no guarantee of anything when it comes to sex. But if he was queer, I doubt that he'd be a regular at the U.T., which hardly seems like it's that kind of a joint."

"Well, with all due respect, Snap, I think I'll go back

to my quiet games of chance down in Englewood. The only violence there is when Benny Kaplan gets pissed off about his lousy cards and throws the deck across the room."

"I don't blame you, Pickles. Clearly, this grand university community with all of its gothic buildings isn't as tranquil as it looks."

The next morning, my head reminded me of the previous night's beer consumption as I sat at my kitchen table with coffee and the *Tribune*. On Page 4, there was a three-paragraph item about Bergman:

U OF CHICAGO PROF
FOUND MURDERED IN
HYDE PARK APARTMENT

The body of a University of Chicago faculty member, Arthur Richard Bergman, was found in his South Cornell Avenue apartment last night after police received an anonymous telephone tip.

Bergman, 41, had been an associate professor of physics at the school for the last eight years, according to a university spokesman. Police said he had been strangled with a rope, and that he apparently had been dead for several days.

The dead man had received his

undergraduate degree from the University of Chicago and a PhD. from the Massachusetts Institute of Technology.

It was bare-bones stuff, although I was surprised Ellis was able to get even that much into the home-delivered editions, given that everything happened fairly late in the evening. And at that, he probably had to rouse a university mouthpiece out of bed to supply some background on poor Bergman.

My head was still hammering when I got to the press room a few minutes before nine. "Anything new on that murder down in Hyde Park after Ellis went home?" I asked Corcoran, our overnight man.

"Nope, just what's in the three-star," he said dismissively, getting up to turn the *Tribune* desk over to me. This was typical of Corcoran. He never went out of his way to advance a story or do any serious digging. The words "enterprise reporting" were not part of his vocabulary, which is why he liked working the graveyard shift, when little news occurred.

The Bergman murder never came up during our start-of-the-day conversation, although when we broke camp to go to our respective beats, Packy Farmer of the *Herald American* stopped me. "Hey, Snap, when you talk to Fahey, make sure you get new stuff on that Hyde Park murder. We're going to need something fresh."

"Yeah, and for us too," Eddie Metz put in. "There

wasn't much in the *Trib*, and I see the *Sun* didn't even bother to run it." He smirked at Dirk O'Farrell.

"You're right, Eddie," O'Farrell snapped. "But the readers of your tabloid rag just suck this kind of thing up. Hand the *Times* a good juicy murder, and its audience is as happy as a bunch of pigs in shit."

"Gentlemen, gentlemen–and I use the term loosely– that's enough bickering," Anson Masters pronounced. "We all, except of course for our Miss Joanie here, have a newspaper to serve, and we need to get to work. And by the way, Mr. Malek, although the *Daily News* does not place a high priority on the baser and more sordid crime stories, we too will be interested in any additional information Mr. Fahey can provide about the unfortunate university murder."

"Okay, Antsy. I'll give the *Times* this, though: They aren't hypocrites, and they don't pretend to be something they aren't, like another and somewhat pompous afternoon paper I could name." I winked at Masters and headed off for Fergus Fahey's office.

"And a hello to you, Mr. Malek of the *Tribune*," Elsie Dugo chirped as I eased into her anteroom. "You look a little tired this morning, if I may say so."

"I can't stop you from saying so. It's a long and complex story," I said, "and one that I'm not up to recounting at the moment. How's his nibs today?" I tilted my head in the direction of Fahey's sanctum.

"He looks better than you do. But I know he's

62

expecting you; go on in."

"Morning, Fergus," I said with forced cheer as I dropped into one of his guest chairs and tossed an opened pack of Lucky Strikes onto his desk within his reach.

"Morning yourself," he muttered, looking up from a sheaf of paperwork. "You don't look so hot."

"Between you and Elsie, I'm going to get a complex. What is it? Did I forget to brush my hair this morning?"

He grunted. "Your hair looks fine. Now about your eyes…" He was interrupted by Elsie's entry. She set a cup of coffee on the corner of the desk closest to me. "Here, you poor baby; there's lots more if you need it."

"Okay, okay," I said, holding up both hands in mock surrender. "So I may have slightly overindulged last evening."

"Slightly?" Elsie laughed, clicking out in her high heels and closing the door behind her before I could mount a response.

"So, what do you think about this Hyde Park business?" I posed to Fahey.

"I was about to ask you the very same question. Funny thing: An anonymous call came in last night about the murder, and not more than fifteen minutes later, my boys tell me that your night man, Ellis, was in here asking for information about the killing. Seems he knew just about as much as we did–and at about the same time."

"Interesting. Just goes to show that civic-minded citizens know enough to call the *Tribune* as well as the

63

Police Department."

"Uh-huh. I'll agree with the 'interesting' part," Fahey muttered, wrinkling a ruddy and ample brow and running a hand across his jaw. "Why do I have a strange feeling that you're somehow involved in this business?"

"Can't imagine, Fergus. Other than the fact that it was you who brought up concerns about Hyde Park to me a few days back. Looks like maybe Grady, your worrywart of a precinct boss down there, had reason to be concerned. What have you found out about this professor's murder?"

"Huh! You mean in all these many hours since the body was found. Very funny. By the way, you said you were going to do a little nosing around down there for us. Find anything out?"

"Haven't had the time–sorry. But back to the murder: Anything turn up that wasn't in our story this morning?"

"Not so far. Of course we're looking into the possibility that it had a homosexual slant."

"So you figure he knew his killer?"

"I guess so," he said, clearly uncomfortable. "That's a world I don't have any experience with, and I plan to keep it that way. Of course, it also could have been a burglary–maybe the killer was trying to force Bergman to tell him where his money was."

"Maybe so," I answered. "But the place didn't look like it had been–" I stopped in mid-sentence, but it was too late.

"Didn't look like *what*?" Fahey spat, coming halfway out of his chair.

"I mean…"

"Just what *do* you mean?"

"Well…I…"

"Dammit, Malek, you were in that apartment last night, weren't you?"

Fahey uses my last name only when he's angry, and this time his red face was a giveaway even before he opened his mouth.

"Uh, I think the caller said something to Ellis about the place not being rifled," I said, trying to recover.

"Oh, horse shit! You've been caught–give it up."

"Hey, I didn't disturb anything. I went in, took one look at the body, and got the hell out."

Fahey's glower was strong enough to cut through a concrete wall. "And how, if I may deign to ask, did you get in there in the first place? And don't tell me the door was ajar. I'm not as stupid as I sometimes seem."

"I had…somebody with me who knows how to work with locks. But Fergus, this was all my idea. He was just doing what I asked him to."

"And I'll bet whoever he is, he's got a rap sheet. Let's see, we've got breaking and entering and disturbing a crime scene, and that's just for starters. I'm sure we can work up some other charges."

"Fergus, look at it this way: If I hadn't gone in there, it might have been days, even weeks, before the poor

65

bastard's body was found. This gives you an earlier start."

Fahey leaned back and crossed beefy arms over his chest, considering me. "I'm not sure I ever believe anything you say, which seems a prudent approach. But what the hell, I'll try it anyway. What made you pick that specific apartment to break into?"

The game was up, and I knew it. I spent the next several minutes telling Fahey how I had visited the U.T. in Hyde Park on a tip–I never mentioned Pickles–and had sat next to a guy at the bar who hinted that he had some sort of mysterious inside information on how we were going to win the war.

"Sounds like a crackpot," Fahey growled. "Universities are full of them, you know, particularly that one." He tilted his head in the general direction of Hyde Park.

"I don't doubt it, although I'll have to take your word for it; I never made it past high school. Anyway, this Bergman disappears–doesn't show up at the bar for days, even though he was apparently an almost-every-night regular. I found out his name from the bartender and got curious, so I went to his place."

"Tell me about the guy who picked the lock."

I held up my hands, palms out. "Uh-uh, Fergus, no can do. He's a regular source for me, and if I gave you his name, he wouldn't be any more."

"Breaking and entering, Malek. Breaking and entering."

"We steered you to a murder. That has to count for something. And besides, I didn't touch anything in the apartment."

"But you wiped your prints off doorknobs and light switches, I'll bet."

"Yes, but–"

"'Yes, but,' my ass. When you wiped those down, you could also have erased the killer's prints."

"Fergus, did you find any prints other than Bergman's in the apartment?"

He scowled. "Way too early to tell. Our guys are still going over the scene."

"You know darn well you won't find any. Whoever it was surely used gloves."

"You've got an answer for everything, don't you?"

"No, I don't. For starters, here are three questions that need answers: Did Bergman really know about something, about some weapon maybe, that could win us the war? And if he did–granted, that's a big if–was he killed because of it? And if so, why?"

"I think you're reading more into this killing than it warrants," Fahey insisted.

"Okay then, let's hear your theory. I think we've already disposed of the burglary idea, unless your boys find out differently as they comb the apartment. But I'll bet you a crisp fin that they'll find Bergman's billfold undisturbed. And, no, before you say something, I did not take a peek inside his wallet. After less than a minute in there, I was ready to throw up. I couldn't get out fast enough."

"Serves you right. Okay, I'll concede the point on burglary, or technically robbery, since it was face-to-face. The guy didn't figure to be loaded, not on an associate professor's salary and living in a three-room flat."

"Okay, Fergus, next, let's go back to the possible homosexual angle. Except for his shirt, Bergman was fully clothed, and he even had an undershirt on. Hardly seems like your typical queer sex crime."

"Could have been just the work of a deranged sadist," he said, pulling a Lucky out of my pack and firing it up.

"Could have been," I agreed. "But why was Bergman the target?"

"Snap, you've been around the police world long enough to know that a lot of killings don't make any sense whatsoever. Maybe the killer saw Bergman in that bar and followed him home. Maybe a student in one of his classes had a grudge. Maybe it was a husband whose wife was having a fling with the professor. Give me twenty minutes and I can come up with a lot more 'maybes.' You know damn well there are hundreds if not thousands of people in this town who don't have all their marbles, and all they need is some minor event to set them off. Maybe it's a snub, an insult, an unintentional jostling on a sidewalk, you name it.

"We had a case several years ago where two guys in a bar on Dearborn Street got in a shouting match over whether there were any buffaloes left in the U.S. One of them snapped. He whipped out a revolver and shot the other one dead, right there on his barstool, like it was the goddamn Wild West. Some actions simply can't be explained."

"Maybe not. But I still think there's a more complex reason for this killing."

"Just don't try to do our work for us, okay?" Fahey growled. "You've muddled things up enough already."

"Come on, you know me, Fergus."

"That's exactly what I'm afraid of."

Chapter 8

Over the next two days, the dailies gave the "Hyde Park Murder" varying degrees of coverage, ranging from the *Times,* with its PROFESSOR GARROTED! screamer, to the resolutely sedate *Daily News*, which ran the Bergman story at the bottom of Page 1 with a headline reading "Police Seek Suspects in University Slaying."

"Exciting stuff, Antsy," Packy Farmer sneered, flipping a copy of the *Daily News* onto the floor next to his desk. "Your editors really know how to make murder sound dull. Or, wait…maybe, just maybe, it's your writing that puts your paper's headline writers to sleep. Could that possibly be?"

Masters cleared his throat. "I can only work with what I am given by our noble comrade here from the *Tribune*," he said, swiveling to face me, palms upturned in a gesture of helplessness.

"Aha," Dirk O'Farrell chimed in. "So our Mr. Masters, who is content–as I fear we all are–to let Brother Malek cover the Detective Bureau for us, now complains that he's not gleaning good material from said Malek. And yet, Mr. Metz here seems to get the story top play in his publication."

"Yes, but his publication is not the *Chicago Daily News*," Masters countered with irritation. He stressed the last three words as if they were worthy of worship.

"Well now, ain't that just the cat's pajamas," Eddie Metz said in a rare burst of self-expression. "Anson, here is one great story, any way you slice it. A prof, or an associate prof–what the hell difference does it really make?–is killed in his apartment right in the middle of a goddamn university community full of wiseheads who have forgotten more than any of us will ever know. An ivy-walled campus is hardly the place you'd expect this sort of thing, right? Of course we're going to give it top-of-the-page play, for God's sake. Seems to me we're in this business to, one, report the news, and two, sell newspapers."

O'Farrell clapped four times, spacing them for effect. "Nicely done, Eddie, nicely done indeed. Didn't know you had it in you. Take that, Anson."

I stayed out of this little go-round, mainly because the *Trib* was in the same boat as the *Daily News*, underplaying the murder with placement off of Page 1 and bland headlines such as "Search Continues for Campus Killer." My editors' lack of interest in the case, however, was no reason for me to slack off. The Bergman funeral was to be held Saturday at a church just off the university campus, and I figured it might be worth my while to slip in and play the anonymous observer.

* * *

The stone church on 57th Street looked solidly traditional to me as I approached it from the east. Being a lapsed Catholic and a nonchurchgoer myself, I have had very few occasions to enter a house of worship, particularly one that is not associated with the Vatican.

The service was scheduled to start in five minutes when I went into the sanctuary at 10:55 and took a seat at the back. Less than two dozen people, almost all of them men, were scattered among the folding chairs in the vaulted Gothic sanctuary, which looked like the interiors of European churches that I had seen in photographs. As viewed from behind, most of the mourners seemed to be in their thirties and forties. There was no casket at the front.

I thought some other reporters might have shown up, but apparently the papers, or at least their editors, had little interest in the murder anymore. We sat in silence–no music–until a tall, gaunt figure strode to the lectern from a door at the front. He wore a baggy black suit, a thin, dark tie, and a somber expression on a long, narrow face with prominent cheekbones. His sparse, reddish hair was combed across his scalp in a futile attempt to forestall the baldness that lurked no more than a half decade away. He peered out at the gathering over horned-rimmed glasses perched on the end of his nose, nodded, and cleared his throat.

"Good morning," he intoned, expressionless, as his

bony fingers gripped the lectern. There was no response.

Another throat-clearing. "We are here this day to pay tribute to the life of Arthur Bergman. A fine gentleman and a fine teacher." More throat noises and a pause.

"I wish that I had known Mr. Bergman," continued the speaker, who never chose to identify himself. "I know, from what I have heard from some of you here"–he dipped his head toward his small audience–"that I would have found him fascinating company, as I know that so many of you did. And I also know you will continue to remember him and his gifted and creative mind.

"In addition to his scientific brilliance, several of you have told me of his unwavering loyalty to this school." He spread his arms wide, turning to his left and then to his right, as if to encompass the entire university. "Not that he agreed with everything that was done here." A slight smile and what passed for a chuckle.

"From what I have been told, he never forgave the school's administration for dropping the football program. He was an avid fan of the team, his team, his Maroons. And at every home game, he could be found cheering from a seat near the fifty-yard line at Stagg Field, a stadium now overrun with weeds."

The speaker–was he a minister?–went on for a few more minutes, talking in platitudes about Bergman as if filling time, which probably was the case. He closed with a rambling prayer about the eternal nature of life and death, and invited everyone to stay for a reception in the social hall downstairs.

We all filed down a stone stairway into a cheerless and dimly lit basement room where two smiling, matronly ladies stood behind a long table with coffee, tea, cakes, cookies, and sandwiches arrayed on it. Hardly like the spirited wakes I had attended, where the drink-mixer was the most popular figure.

I stood at the rear of the room, surveying the gathering. There were only two women, one a striking, willowy blonde who would turn heads in any setting and who, I later learned, had been Bergman's second wife. The other, a generation older, turned out to be an aunt from Minneapolis. The balance of the assemblage of less than twenty were men, most of whom looked to be contemporaries of the deceased. They were a varied lot, several in herringbone sport coats that apparently were a popular uniform on the campus, and a few of them sporting beards.

After everyone else was served, I stepped to the table and got coffee and a plate of cookies. As I was biting into the first one, a short gent with a bushy brown mustache flecked with gray and a black turtleneck sweater introduced himself.

"Hello, I'm Nate Lazar, I worked with Arthur in the department," he said, holding out a hand, which I dutifully shook. He cocked his head, studying me. "Don't believe I've met you before. Are you a relative of his?"

"No...no, I didn't really know him all that well, but

we had drinks together in the University Tavern a few times," I said, exaggerating the number of occasions I had met him. "We had some interesting conversations."

"Ah, yes, Arthur liked to drop in at the U.T. with some frequency. So...you're not associated with the university?"

"No, I'm..." I paused, wondering what tack to take, then decided to hell with it, why pussyfoot around? "...I'm a newspaper reporter with the *Tribune*. Name's Malek. Steve Malek."

"Really?" He turned and carefully set his coffee cup on the table. "Are you covering Arthur's...death?"

"Not officially. I came down here originally because we at the paper had heard rumors of unrest in Hyde Park. I stopped by the U.T. to look around and get a feel for the neighborhood, and that's where I met Mr. Bergman. Just happened to sit next to him at the bar."

Lazar raised his eyebrows. "What kind of unrest would that be?"

"It was sort of vague," I told him. "We never got any specifics."

He nodded absently. "I should introduce you to some of Arthur's other colleagues in the Physics Department, if you don't mind."

I said I didn't, and he led me over to three men who stood in a circle talking at the far end of the room.

"Mr....Malek, isn't it? I'd like you to meet these gentlemen. This is Theodore Ward, Edward Rickman, and Miles Overby."

I shook hands with each as Lazar told them I was a *Tribune* reporter. Their faces registered varying degrees of surprise, interest, and reservation. Overby, rawboned with dark hair parted in the center and wearing rimless glasses, spoke first. "So, I take it you are here because of the…er, the nature of Arthur's death?" His tone was disapproving.

"Not entirely. As I was telling Mr. Lazar a minute ago, I had met Mr. Bergman a couple of times at the University Tavern. We happened to sit next to each other at the bar and got to talking, the way people often do in saloons."

"Mr. Malek had come down here because he had gotten word of 'unrest' in Hyde Park," Lazar put in.

"Unrest, eh? Of what sort?" It was Theodore Ward, bald, double-chinned, and stocky, the vest of his tweedy suit straining to contain his stomach.

I shrugged. "As I was also telling Mr. Lazar, we never got specifics. I thought I'd take a look around, and that's when I met Mr. Bergman in the saloon."

"What did you talk about?" asked Rickman, who could have been a model for a men's-store newspaper ad. He had sandy hair and a square jaw and was the best-dressed man in the room, his double-breasted blue blazer worn with a blue-and-white striped shirt and a silver silk tie.

"We didn't even talk at first," I told him. "He was in

a conversation with the man on the other side of him. The subject was the war. The other guy was pretty glum about how things have been going, but Bergman seemed absolutely convinced that we would win. No doubt whatsoever. Everybody these days should be as confident as he was. It impressed me."

They all leaned in as I talked, eyes fastened on me and apparently waiting for the next words out of my mouth. I felt it was time for a change of venue.

"How about our continuing this gathering with something stronger than church coffee?" I proposed, looking down at my cup. "Let's reconvene at the U. T. My watch says it's just past noon, so we can't be accused of being morning drinkers. And I'm buying."

"Sounds good to me," said Nate Lazar, but the others appeared dubious, probably not anxious to be the guests, even for a drink, of someone who toiled in the lowly ranks of journalism.

"Oh, come on, boys," Lazar joshed. "Let's at least hoist a glass with Mr. Malek. We certainly don't want him to think we're unfriendly down here, now, do we?"

Lazar was so amiable that he broke whatever tension had been building, and after the four said their goodbyes and gave their condolences to others in the room, we lumbered up the dark stairway, destination, University Tavern.

Chapter 9

As we walked east and north toward the tavern, I fell into conversation with Edward Rickman while the other three talked among themselves, mostly about their remembrances of Bergman. Rickman seemed intrigued by my interest in the murder.

"So, Mr. Malek, is it typical for a reporter to go to a funeral in a situation like this? I must confess to being unfamiliar with the workings of journalists." His tone, like Overby's earlier at the church, was tinged with disapproval, with a possible dash of academic snobbery thrown in.

"No two cases are the same, but it's not out of the ordinary," I responded.

"Why? Whatever would you expect to learn?" Contentiousness had now crept into his voice.

"Hard to say."

"I should think so. Unless I'm not as observant as I like to think, I didn't notice any police lurking at the church. And if anybody might be expected to seek clues, or suspects, at a funeral service, it would seem to be them."

"Good point," I answered, refusing to be drawn into an argument as we arrived at the University Tavern.

The place was almost empty. We found a circular table in a corner big enough to accommodate five, and a waitress with a weary expression and a yellow pencil behind one ear took our orders. Rickman ordered scotch and water, Overby a bourbon highball, the rest of us beer.

"I'm puzzled as to why you wanted to meet with us, Mr. Malek, although I've never been known to turn down a beer," Lazar said with a chuckle.

"I gather you all worked with Mr. Bergman and were close to him, right?"

"As close as anyone could be to Arthur," Rickman put in. "He was something of a loner. But all four of us here, plus Arthur, joined the faculty at about the same time, so we became something of a support group for one another, complaining about university policies and other faculty members, the sort of griping that's typical of professors everywhere."

"Of the five of us, though," Ward added, "Arthur was the least open. He tended to hold his own counsel more than the rest of us. And we had seen less of him lately, as he'd taken this semester off from teaching except for one class."

"Why was that?" I asked.

"He said he was working on some sort of research paper, but he wouldn't talk much about it," Overby said. "Again, that was typical of him–always a touch of mystery."

"This is just a long shot, but I thought one of you might have some idea as to what could have happened," I said.

"Mr. Malek, it won't surprise you to learn that all of us here, along with just about everybody else in the Physics Department down to the secretaries, have been questioned extensively by the police," Rickman said.

"No, that doesn't surprise me at all. But I wouldn't be a good reporter if I didn't ask questions, even if they're the same ones the cops asked."

"Meaning that to you, as well as to the police, we are suspects, is that it?" Ward murmured, lighting his pipe and taking a puff as the drinks were delivered.

I held up a hand, smiling. "Not at all–not in the least. But you might know if he had any enemies, anyone who..." I let the sentence hang, and Rickman finished it: "...might want to kill him?"

Overby took a sip of his highball and leaned forward. "Mr. Malek, I'd like to pose a question of my own: If I understand correctly, you don't have any idea what kind of unrest it was that brought you down here to Hyde Park in the first place, right?"

I saw no reason to be mysterious. "Not really, only that some people living near the campus told police they saw more strangers around the neighborhood, some of them 'foreign-looking.'"

Overby allowed himself a slight smile. "Foreign-looking, eh? I've been on this campus for more than fifteen years, and during that time every third person I've passed on the sidewalks would be termed foreign-looking by the little old ladies living in the big old places up on Woodlawn and University and Kenwood. I can't believe that they're getting worked up about it after all these years."

"It's probably because of the war," I told him. "We're finding that everybody's more nervous now, more suspicious. Hardly surprising."

"But maybe there *are* things going on here," Rickman said. "A lot of us have been doing some wondering of our own."

Ward set his beer down. "Now Ed, let's not get…"

"Let me finish, Theo," Rickman snapped, holding up a palm and turning toward me. "Mr. Malek, have you ever heard of Enrico Fermi?"

"Uh… I don't believe so. Should I?"

"He won a Nobel Prize in physics three, four years ago. One of the great scientific minds today. How about Leo Szilard?" I shook my head.

"Another brilliant physicist," Rickman proclaimed. "Hungarian-born, studied in Berlin, collaborated with Albert Einstein on several projects, developed an electron microscope, got out of Germany before the start of the war. I could go on and on."

"I'll take your word for all of it. So…?"

"So, Mr. Malek…both Fermi and Szilard are on this

82

campus right now. I've seen both of them several times."

I took a healthy swig of beer and wiped my mouth. "Should I be surprised? From what I've been told, this is a great university. Why shouldn't great brains be here?"

Rickman sighed, as if disappointed by my denseness. "They should," he said, "but not in a place called the Metallurgical Laboratory."

"Which I assume means it has something to do with metals."

"So one would think," Theodore Ward said, tugging his vest down over his expansive midsection. "But the 'Met Lab,' as it's commonly known around here, seems like an unlikely place for two of the greatest physicists in the world. On top of that, it's an open secret that there are people from DuPont on the campus. You may know that the company started out as a manufacturer of high explosives."

"Okay, then what's the explanation?" I asked, looking at each of them in turn. I was tired of guessing games, especially when I had to play them with a quartet who probably qualified as geniuses, at least in their field.

Miles Overby cleared his throat. "We–at least some of us–think the Met Lab's a cover for something else. Mr. Malek, have you ever heard of nuclear fission?"

"I feel like I'm a contestant on 'Twenty Questions,' and not doing very damn well at it," I told him. "I have no idea what nuclear fission is, but I suspect you're going to tell me."

"I wouldn't begin trying to explain it," Overby said. "And I don't mean that as an insult by any means. It's a complex concept, but one of the end results is frighteningly simple: An explosive device more powerful and more terrifying than anything the planet has ever seen."

"That sounds melodramatic," I answered, playing my role as the skeptical newspaperman.

"Miles and I disagree on a lot of issues, both inside the world of physics and outside, but on this, he's right, of course," Ward pronounced quietly. "For years, there have been experiments, many of them in secret, on the possible creation of a nuclear weapon. And as Miles says, such a weapon would dwarf anything now in the arsenal of any military force–American, German, Japanese, British, Soviet."

I wasn't through being skeptical. "If the experiments have been so secret, how do you know about them?"

"In the international physics community," Ward said, "it's hard to keep anything from leaking out. For instance, it's widely known that the Germans have been working for the last several years on a nuclear bomb."

"And our government knows about this?"

"Absolutely," Rickman chimed in. "There's no way they *couldn't* know. I'm sure the U.S. has spies everywhere, and so does everybody else in this war, for that matter."

"So that brings us back here to Chicago," I said.

"What's going on here, and what does it have to do with Arthur Bergman's killing?"

"That's what we would all like to know," Lazar piped up, finishing his beer with a slurp. "If work is going forward here on some sort of a weapon, we're not hearing anything, right?" The others nodded.

"The lid is on tight," Ward said through clenched teeth. "And what is terrifying, really terrifying, is that if a weapon really is being developed here–which seems to me very likely–it's being done in the heart of a metropolis of three million people, plus many hundreds of thousands more in the environs. If, God forbid, a mistake is made, this entire city could be wiped out." He snapped his fingers for emphasis.

"Maybe that's the price that we have to pay in wartime," I suggested, not totally believing it. "But if none of you know what's really going on in that Met Lab, what makes you think Arthur Bergman did? And if he did know, why was he killed? And by whom?"

"That's what we're all wondering," Rickman said. "Exactly what did Arthur say to you?"

My answer combined what Pickles had overheard and what Bergman said to me: "He told me something big was happening on the campus that was going to change the world, and when I pressed him, he simply said 'You don't know what I know,' or words to that effect. Then he clammed up." I left out his cryptic comment about "where we will rise again."

"Arthur always had a flair for the dramatic," Lazar put in. "It's questionable how much information he really had."

"We'll never know," Ward said, stating the obvious. "If he had inside sources as to what was going on over at the Met Lab, he surely never shared them with me."

"Or me, either, and I suspect the same is true of the others here as well," Overby said, looking around the table. Lazar and Rickman nodded.

Rickman turned to me. "Do you know the person Arthur was talking to at the bar? The one who was so pessimistic about the war?"

"Never saw him before," I responded truthfully, neglecting to mention that I hadn't seen him at all. And Pickles never told me what he looked like, so I couldn't have described him even if I had wanted to.

"Well, it's in the hands of the police now anyway," Lazar said.

"Or the FBI," Ward added glumly. "But before some law-enforcement outfit finds out who did this, we may all be blown to smithereens."

"Now look who has a flair for the dramatic," Overby chuckled dryly.

"Well, how do *you* feel about nuclear experiments going on in one of the most densely populated cities in the country?" Ward snorted.

"We don't know for certain that these experiments are actually under way," Overby countered.

"Then kindly explain Fermi's presence on the campus. And Szilard's."

Overby said nothing, and the table fell silent. "How about another round?" I ventured, pulling out my billfold. "Remember, these are on me."

"Thanks anyway, but I've got a lunch date with a colleague," Ward said, and the others all told me they, too, had engagements.

As they rose to leave, Lazar pumped my hand. "Mr. Malek, I'm afraid we've availed ourselves of your hospitality and then wasted your time today. We haven't been a lot of help to you."

"Maybe not as far as Arthur's murder is concerned," Ward said. "But we've alerted him to a terrible peril the city is facing. And I would hope he would pass it along to his newspaper."

"What's the *Tribune* going to do, Ted?" Rickman challenged. "Even assuming a bomb really is being built under our noses, the paper has to tread lightly after what happened earlier this year with the Japanese code."

"We were cleared on that by a federal grand jury," I piped up, defending my employer against a claim that the *Tribune* had violated the espionage act by reporting that the code used by the Japanese armed forces had been broken.

"Okay, point taken," Rickman conceded, "but even without that episode, I can't believe the paper would want to report on an American weapon being developed in secret. Hardly a patriotic act."

"Besides, such a revelation might make the university look good," Ward said. "And with all due respect to our journalist friend here, the *Tribune* and its Colonel McCormick are hardly friends of the school. They see us, from President Hutchins himself on down, as a bunch of rabid left-wingers who would like to establish a Communist state on the Midway and undermine all that is good and decent in the American way of life."

"I don't think this bombast is getting us anywhere," Lazar said with a forced smile. "Let's wish Mr. Malek well and hope that he, or the police, find out who killed Arthur, and why. And again, sir, thank you for the drinks and for your concern about our colleague. Please let us know if you find anything out. Or if there is anything we can help you with."

I told them I would stay in touch, which seemed like the polite thing to say. We all left the saloon, which had begun to fill up with the Saturday student crowd–a group that had no football game to attend on this autumn afternoon.

Chapter 10

I got to the Police Headquarters press room a few minutes before 9:00 a.m. on Monday, which is early for me. But Joanie, the City News Bureau reporter, was already there; she was always the first member of the day side to be at her desk. She was young and enthusiastic, while those of us on the papers were, well…older and somewhat less enthusiastic, maybe even a trifle jaded.

She already had her *Tribune* open and was paging through it. She would tackle the *Sun* next, and would get to the early editions of the afternoon papers later. As the other reporters straggled in, she said, "Interesting, very interesting. I never heard of this guy."

"Who's that?" Packy Farmer asked as he finished rolling one of his pathetic little smokes and contemplated it through narrowed eyes.

"Man who used to work for City News," she said. "Years back. The *Trib* obit calls him a legend."

"Not Steel Trap Bascomb?" Anson Masters asked.

"Yeah, that's him. It says here that he got his nickname because of his great memory. Never forgot a story, or a name."

89

"I knew him a little," Masters said. "He was never a regular here at Headquarters, but he filled in occasionally. Seemed like a decent sort, a bit on the quiet side. But my God, what a memory, just as the obit says. He could remember cases from twenty, thirty years earlier, right down to the names of the arresting officers and the detectives and the lawyers. Had the best mind for detail of anybody I ever saw in this business."

"Never ran into him myself," Dirk O'Farrell put in. "And he was probably around before your time, eh, Snap?"

"Actually, I did know him, mainly after his retirement," I answered, not wanting to go into detail. Four years earlier, I had occasion to visit Lemuel "Steel Trap" Bascomb at his house in Oak Park. I was quietly digging up background information on Lloyd Martindale, a potential reform candidate for mayor of Chicago who had been murdered. Even in a state of senility, Steel Trap had lucid moments, and he remembered events from years earlier that helped explain why Martindale had been bumped off.

Indeed, Steel Trap had been part of a chapter in my checkered newspaper career. I came close to getting a scoop on the Martindale case and subsequent events–including three other deaths–but that's another story. It's one I had never shared with the others in the Headquarters press room, since I didn't deal them in on my digging.

Joanie continued reading the *Trib* obituary. "It says

90

this Steel Trap guy was with City News for thirty-nine years. If he was supposed to be so darn good, why didn't he end up working for one of the dailies?"

I waited for Masters to respond, but he just shrugged. Joanie turned toward me. "Couldn't tell you," I said, although I knew Steel Trap had felt the dailies killed stories that reflected badly on their advertisers, and he couldn't abide that. I had learned that from his daughter.

His daughter. I hadn't seen Catherine Reed in more than four years, not since my last visit to Steel Trap. I had almost called her two or three times, but always held off...I can't explain why.

I read the obituary in my own copies of The *Tribune* and the *Sun*. They both gave it nice play, and the *Trib* had a picture of him that must have been taken before World War I. There was to be a visitation in Oak Park that night.

After wrapping up an uneventful day at Headquarters, I hopped a northbound streetcar and grabbed a quick supper at a Harding's in the Loop, then took the Lake Street Elevated west to Oak Park. The mortuary was just two blocks from an El stop in the town's main business district.

I hadn't expected a large gathering, even with the extensive obituaries in all the papers, and I was right. About a half dozen people were clustered at the front of the parlor near the casket. Catherine, wearing a simple black dress, had her back to me as she talked to an elderly couple.

I've never been a fan of open caskets, and here was yet another reason why. Even the undertakers couldn't do much for poor old Steel Trap. He hadn't been in all that good shape when I'd seen him a few years ago, but the end of his life had not been kind. His face, even after the embalmers' efforts, had shrunk to beyond what I remembered, and his skin made him seem like a wax museum exhibit.

I stood before the casket, thinking back to my visits with Steel Trap and his struggles with questions about events from decades earlier–questions he once would have answered without a pause. I started to turn away when I felt a hand on my sleeve.

"Hello, Steve," she said softly. "It's very nice of you to come." She looked as fresh-faced and appealing as she had been those years ago, and I wondered yet again why I had walked away from what seemed like a relationship with so much promise.

"I was so sorry to hear about…" I let it hang, turning my palms up. People have called me glib, but none of them have ever seen me at a visitation or a wake. If there's a right thing to say, I've never found it.

"Thank you, Steve. These last months have been particularly bad for Daddy. I finally had to move him to a nursing home." She teared up, but took in a couple of deep breaths and composed herself.

"I'm sure that you had no choice."

"I simply couldn't take care of him anymore. Twice he wandered away from the house, and one time the police found him more than six blocks away, sitting on a curb and holding his head in his hands, muttering something about having to get to the Criminal Courts Building in the city to cover a case. It might be sacrilegious to call this a blessing, but Steve, I'm not saying that because of myself. I never felt that caring for him was an imposition. It's just that his safety became an issue."

"You made the right decision, Catherine, as hard as it had to be for you."

She nodded. "Two weeks ago, he slipped into a coma, and the doctor told me that he'd never come out of it, which turned out to be true. He was six weeks short of his 76th birthday."

"That's a damn good run," I told her. "You have a lot to be proud of. He was one hell of a guy. He deserved the play the papers gave him today."

"Thank you, Steve. He really did have a good run. You know, he was born the year after Lincoln was shot. And one of his earliest memories–he told us this story many times at home–was of watching the Chicago Fire. His parents had a place on the Far North Side of the city, it was really almost out in the country then. From where they lived, they could see the flames and red sky to the south, and smell the smoke. It made quite an impact on a five-year-old."

"Well, I was glad for the chance to have met him, even though he'd…slowed down a good deal by then."

"And I know he really enjoyed your visits, too. They seemed to perk him up quite a bit. I'll never forget that night at dinner when you swapped those crazy stories about the pickpockets who each had six fingers on one hand."

"Crazy stories, but true. I enjoyed those visits, too. I'm only sorry I didn't make more of them. Are you still working at the local public library?"

"You've got a good memory," she said with a hint of a smile. "When Daddy's situation got really bad, I took a leave of absence, but after he went into the nursing home, I went back to working three days a week. When the head librarian heard about Daddy's death, she said she'd like to have me on the staff full-time. So that starts after the first of the year, and I'm very happy about it. It's a pleasant place to work."

"That is wonderful news," I said, meaning it. "I think it's worthy of a celebration. And I can think of no better way to celebrate than with a dinner. What about next weekend?"

She gave me a look that I interpreted as half puzzled and half surprised. "A sympathy meal, Steve? I appreciate the gesture, I really do, but it's not necessary. Thank you, though."

"Catherine, it is not a sympathy gesture," I said, starting to raise my voice but then lowering it as another couple entered the parlor and started walking toward us. "I think it would be nice for us to get together."

"I'm not sure…"

I grinned. "Say yes, or I'll cause a scene, right here, right now." That brought a full-fledged smile, along with the hint of a blush, unless I was flattering myself.

"I'll…all right, call me and we'll set up a time. And Steve…thank you." She took my hand and squeezed it, then turned to greet more arriving mourners. I took a last look at the remains of Steel Trap Bascomb and vowed that when my time to depart drew near, I would insist upon cremation.

Chapter 11

The next morning, I had been at my desk in the headquarters press room for only five minutes when I got a call from the *Tribune's* South Side police reporter, Al MacAfee.

"Snap, I need a favor from you, a big one."

"Okay, what have you gone and done, Mac? Do I have to bail you out? Were you caught in a crap game? Or a raid on a brothel?"

"No, no, you know me better than that." He sounded flustered.

I did indeed know MacAfee fairly well. He was honest, earnest, hard-working, and a decent, thorough young reporter, if somewhat on the excitable side.

"Okay, try me," I said. "Of course I make no guarantees."

"Of course not, Snap, I wouldn't expect you to. Well, here's the situation: My wife, Flora–I think you may have met her at a party one time a couple of years back– anyway, Flora has been pregnant for seven months. She's been having a lot of problems with this one–it's our second. The first one, Liam, he's almost two now, was a breeze. But this time, it's been rough right from the start."

"Sorry to hear that, Mac. But where do I come in?"

"I think you know that we live in Rogers Park, Snap, almost to the Evanston border. It takes me more than an hour to get from our apartment to even the nearest South Side precinct, Hyde Park. Streetcar, Elevated, Illinois Central train–most days my commute, morning and evening, is three hours, sometimes a little more."

"Go on."

"Well, the doctor doesn't think Flora should be alone for almost twelve hours every day, not the way things have been going."

"Why don't you come to the point, Mac."

"Well…I was wondering if you might be willing, just for two months to, well, to switch places. I swear, Snap, I'm not looking to take over your beat. But if we could swap, just temporarily, it would cut my time away from home by more than one hour, maybe closer to two. And you live a lot farther south than I do, so it wouldn't be a great imposition for you."

"Have you talked to anybody else about this?"

"Not a soul. I know it would have to be approved by Mr. Maloney himself, but I wanted to ask you first. If you don't want to do it, I'll try something else."

"South police, eh? I haven't done it in years, not since '29 or '30. You still divide your time among the Hyde Park, Englewood, Grand Crossing, Gresham, and Kensington station houses?"

"Pretty much, with occasional swings by Chicago Lawn, Deering, and South Chicago. But I spend most days at Hyde Park and cover the other precincts from there."

"And why not–better restaurants, right? And better transportation downtown?"

"Well, yes. And nicer cops, by and large. What do you think, Snap?" MacAfee sounded tense.

"In my very limited experience with him, Pat Maloney seems like a pretty decent guy, as managing editors go. He's no Edward Scott Beck, but then who is? They threw away the mold with Beck. Tell Maloney that it's jake by me if we do a two-month switch, and I'll bet you three-to-one that he gives it his stamp. Let me know what he says."

MacAfee let out a sigh. "Thank you, Snap, thank you. I will call Mr. Maloney tomorrow."

"Mac, you are aware, are you not, that you will be spending a good deal of time seeking information in the office of Homicide Chief Fergus Fahey?"

"Uh, yeah, I guess so. I do know that you guys hit it off pretty well."

"That's because I work at it. Fahey can be a tough customer sometimes, but always fair. And he loves Lucky Strike smokes, if you get my drift."

"I do. I smoke Camels, but I'm willing to change."

"Good strategy. And there's a reward. When you're in his office, which will be often, you will be drinking the

99

very best coffee in the building, brewed by the comely and charming Elsie Dugo, Fahey's Girl Friday. But you're a married joe, so her appearance shouldn't matter to you, right?"

"Uh, right, absolutely right." MacAfee was a good man, but he didn't have much sense of humor, and he didn't know when he was being kidded. I knew he'd do fine if Maloney okayed the switch. I wasn't worried that Mac would try to take over the Headquarters beat permanently. The truth is though, that I might not have been so willing to make the switch if I hadn't come across this Bergman business. This seemed like a good time to be a reporter in Hyde Park.

The next day, a little before noon, I got a phone call in the Headquarters press room from J. Loy "Pat" Maloney, who had been managing editor of the *Trib* since 1939, when he took over the post on the death of Bob Lee.

"Mr. Malek," he said, "I understand from Alvin MacAfee that you have agreed to switch beats with him during the last weeks of his wife's difficult pregnancy. Is that the case?"

"Yes, sir."

"Well, I must say that's very generous of you. This is a little out of the ordinary, but I met with the city editor, and he has no objections. And neither do I."

"I'm happy to help Mac, Mr. Maloney," I told him,

hoping he would remember my gesture the next time I requested assignment as a war correspondent.

"Good, good. After the baby comes, you can of course return to Headquarters. Everyone seems happy with your work, and I hear, again from the city editor, that you have particularly good sources in the Homicide area."

"I like to think so. And one of the things I plan to do on Mac's first day is to introduce him to Fergus Fahey and get him set up there."

"Excellent, I'm glad to hear it! I know he can count on you to show him the ropes."

So it was that two days later, I introduced Mac to all the members of the Headquarters press room and told them about the switch.

"Hah! Don't give us that 'temporary' hogwash, Snap," Packy Farmer gibed. "The truth is that the high muckety-mucks up in Tribune Tower finally caught on to your slothful ways and decided to replace you with this fine young fellow. He will indeed be a welcome addition to our intrepid band of warriors."

"Mac," I said, putting an arm over his shoulder, "beware of this questionable specimen. He will be all over you for information every time you come back from Fahey's office. He can't even spell 'homicide' without my help.

"This room is a den of rogues and rascals," I went on, "with the exception of this fine lady, Joanie, who nobly represents the City News Bureau of Chicago. Would that these reprobates had her dedication to duty and to the high principles that exemplify our profession."

"Quick, get the man a soapbox," Dirk O'Farrell rasped. "He's delivering one of his sermons."

"You wouldn't know a sermon if you heard one, Dirk," I riposted. "I'll wager you haven't seen the inside a church in thirty years. Come, Mac, let us leave these knaves to their nefarious devices and call upon the estimable Chief of Detectives, Fergus Sean Fahey."

We went down two floors and stepped into Fahey's small anteroom, occupied as usual by Elsie Dugo. "Hello, you vision of loveliness. Is the high panjandrum in his sanctum?"

"Watch your tongue around here, mister," she sassed. "We don't allow that kind of language. Who's your good-looking friend?"

"This, Miss Dugo, is Alvin MacAfee, an outstanding and intrepid reporter who is going to be replacing me for the next several weeks while I go on a super-secret spy mission. You must promise to be polite to him at all times."

"Hah! I'm always polite–at least to those who are polite to me," she said with a smirk.

"I'll remember that. Can you announce us to his eminence?"

Elsie gave a toss of her head. "Mr. Malek and a gentleman to see you," she pronounced into her intercom.

"I believe the proper phrasing is 'Mr. Malek and *another* gentleman,'" I tossed off as we went into Fahey's cluttered office.

"Morning, Fergus, I'd like to have you meet Alvin MacAfee, known at the paper as Mac. He's going to be the *Tribune's* man here for the next several weeks."

"So they finally got wise to you," Fahey said, rising and shaking Mac's hand.

"Funny, that's about what the others in the press room said, too," I replied, trying to sound hurt. "This is only temporary, honest it is, but you'll find Mac to be a first-rate reporter. Try to treat him with more respect than you've treated me over the years."

"And you say that after all I've done for you," Fahey fired back, dropping into his chair and turning his palms up. "All the exclusives I've handed to you on a platter."

"No need to go on, Fergus. I've already told Mac all about you."

Fahey nodded. "Then he must know my favorite smokes are–"

"Luckies," Mac snapped, whipping a pack out of his pocket and slapping it down on Fahey's blotter.

"This boy has promise, no doubt about it," the chief said, beaming. "So, Snap, what's to become of you while this fine gentleman fills your chair?"

"We're doing a temporary swap, Fergus. I'll be covering the South Side police beat."

"Really?" Fahey's Irish face registered interest.

"Mind if I ask whose idea this is?"

I turned to MacAfee. "It's mine, Chief Fahey," he said earnestly.

"Call me Fergus."

"It's my idea, Fergus," he repeated, going on to explain the situation with his wife's pregnancy. "And when I proposed the swap to Steve, he was good enough to go along with it. I really appreciate that."

"Wonderful fellow, this Malek is," Fahey said with a benevolent smile as he leaned back with his hands laced behind his head. "Always thinking of others, he is."

"Well, he surely has helped me," Mac said, apparently oblivious to Fahey's sarcasm. "And I'm really looking forward to this assignment."

"I'm sure we're going to get along just fine," the grizzled cop said, reaching into the pack of newly arrived Luckies and pulling one out. "And now, if you don't mind, Mr…MacAfee, is it? I'd like to have a few words privately with the man you're replacing. Some unfinished business."

"Sure. And I look forward to working with you," Mac said as he went out and closed the door behind him.

"So," Fahey said, leaning back and clasping his hands behind his head, "this swap of yours really was the kid's idea?"

"You heard him, Fergus. He's not the sort to go telling tales."

"Seems interesting though, that you'll be down Hyde

Park way a lot, what with your interest in that prof's murder."

"Chalk it up to coincidence. By the way, anything new on the case?"

Fahey shook his head and took a drag on his Lucky. "Not a blessed thing. My men have talked to damn near everyone on that campus, from professors to secretaries to an ex-wife to both the day and night barkeeps at the University Tavern, and if Bergman had any enemies, nobody's talking. Seems he was something of a loner. Had been married and divorced twice. The other ex-wife lives in California. We've also talked to a lot of people in his apartment building, and hardly any of them knew him more than to just say hello in the hallway or on the stairs. The only one who had even talked to him much was an old spinster who lived down the hall. Said he was a quiet gentle fellow and a good listener. My man said she was very garrulous, so maybe the poor bastard never got a word in edgewise when they did meet.

"But why am I bothering to tell you all this? I'm sure you've been doing plenty of freelance investigating on your own. I should be asking you the questions."

"Well, I have talked to a handful of his colleagues, but with about the same success as you've had. There's one thing that came out, though, although it may not relate to the killing. Maybe your men heard it, too."

"Oh? Try me."

I helped myself to a Lucky from the pack. "There

105

seems to be a suspicion among some of his colleagues that some sort of secret weapon could be in the works right down there on the Midway. You'll remember I mentioned something similar to you right after the murder."

"Yes, I remember. But our men haven't heard about anything like that from the people they've talked to. Besides, that's outside of my jurisdiction. If this is confidential war-effort stuff, we're not about to mess with it."

"Even if it's related to Bergman's murder?"

Fahey leaned back and drew in air. "I'd have to know more about it. Are you telling me everything you've got?"

"Cross my heart."

"Well, there's a switch, if true. Newshound tells all to copper."

"That's me, Fergus. Honest to a fault."

"Yeah, right. Let me give you some advice, Snap."

"Shoot."

"It may have been his idea, but I know damn well that you let this MacAfee kid pull a swap because you want to sniff around down there at the university. Don't bother denying it and don't get in our way. But be careful. The Bergman murder may be strictly a private thing, but if there is a connection to some kind of weapons development–notice I said if–you could find yourself in far deeper trouble than you bargained for."

"I appreciate your concern."

"I mean it, Snap. This war has changed the rules, changed everything. You've seen it everywhere. Places that are all of a sudden 'off limits' to civilians. The Number One priority is winning the war, period. It's more important than putting mobsters behind bars, than catching kidnappers, than nailing murderers. That doesn't mean we're going to stop doing our jobs, not by any means. But there's been a shift of priorities, and sometimes we have to go along with the war effort. Quote me and I'll deny I ever said any of this. But by God, Snap, be careful–it's a new world out there."

"Thanks for the advice, Fergus. I really mean that." If only I had followed it.

Chapter 12

In my years at Headquarters, I had forgotten what it was like to be without a home base, an office. And at the beginning, I missed it. The first week on the South beat, I dutifully visited each of the precincts in the area, introducing myself to the district commanders and, more important, to the desk sergeants, the ones who really kept the operations going. After a few days, I settled in and made the Hyde Park station my home base, much as MacAfee had.

There were three reasons: (1) the proximity to both the Illinois Central rail line from downtown and to convenient restaurants; (2) the ongoing Bergman murder investigation in the neighborhood; and (3) the presence of Mark Waldron as desk sergeant at Hyde Park.

Waldron was a "desk sergeant's desk sergeant," a gentleman copper who, unlike many of his brethren, actually seemed to like newspaper men and always let us use the police phones to call other precincts. Some of the less-friendly desk men barred us from the free phones, which meant we dropped our nickels into the pay phones to call other stations or the newspaper. I remembered

Waldron from years earlier, and I was delighted to see him when I walked into the station house on Lake Park Avenue my first day on the beat.

"Well, if it isn't Snap Malek in the flesh," Waldron proclaimed from behind the front desk. "Haven't seen you in some time, but you haven't changed much. Including that snap brim hat, which if memory serves is how you landed your moniker, correct?"

"Correct, Sergeant. And I must say you're looking well yourself. I assume you credit that to clean living?"

"Lord knows I try, and I get a lot of help on the home front. What brings you down our way?"

"I'm filling in for MacAfee. His wife's having a rough pregnancy, so we agreed to switch beats for a few weeks."

Waldron leaned his elbows on the counter and nodded. "He's a good lad, hard-working, and I've heard a bit about the troubles at home. Nice that you're filling in."

"How are things here nowadays?"

He took a sip from his coffee cup and shrugged. "About the same as ever. Quiet most of the time, but a little busier Friday and Saturday nights, as you'd expect, mostly because of booze. A guy in a bar or at a fraternity party gets a snootful, and the next thing you know, punches are thrown and we end up tossing somebody, or a bunch of somebodies, into the lockup. You know the drill."

"I do. Although you also had that murder down here

the other night."

"Oh yeah, the U of C prof. Doesn't sound like the boys downtown have gotten very far toward solving that one."

"That's what I've heard. Then there was that concern about a lot of foreigners hanging around the neighborhood."

Waldron smiled and leaned forward, lowering his voice. "This didn't come from me, okay?"

I nodded.

"We got three different calls about what they termed 'strange looking men' in the neighborhood, and the man in the big office here–"

"Grady?"

"Uh-huh. He got concerned about it and apparently mentioned it to higher-ups in a meeting."

"That's gotten around."

"Sure, you'd know, being up at 11th and State at the time. Anyway, the lieutenant, as you may be aware, tends to be a bit quick on the draw sometimes."

"I'm aware of it."

"Well, in this case, he didn't look carefully at the reports. Here's what happened: Three different people called the station and reported seeing 'strange-looking foreigners.' It turns out that all three were women, two of them widows, and all three living in big old houses on the same block of Dorchester north of the Midway. The 'foreigners' turned out to be only one guy, an exotic-looking fellow wearing a turban. He was a visiting professor or scholar or some such from India, and every day he walked down their block from where he was staying, on his way to the campus."

"Much ado about nothing."

"To be sure. And to top it off, only one of the women had seen him originally. Then she called two neighbors and suggested that all three of them call us."

"Just what you need."

"True, but it's hard to be too critical of them. These ladies, and there are thousands of them peeking out from behind their lace curtains on the streets of the city's neighborhoods, are like a second police force. I'll take them any day, even though sometimes they overreact."

"Good point, Sergeant. How is Grady going to change his tune about all this?"

"Oh, I suspect he'll find a way. You might ask him yourself what the current status is concerning suspicious-looking people in the precinct."

"Now that sounds like a capital idea. Thanks for the suggestion."

Waldron smiled wryly. "Just as long as the good lieutenant doesn't know where the suggestion came from."

"He won't. And thanks."

"Don't mention it. And I really mean that."

Being back on the streets again after years at a desk in the 11th and State press room was something of a novelty at the beginning, but I'd rather it had been during the warm-weather months. Although I spent most of my time at the Hyde Park station, I dutifully made the rounds of the other South Side precincts periodically, and they're widely separated. This meant hitching rides in squad cars or resorting to taxis, which were not always easy to find on biting and windy November days.

All that aside, the work itself was a change of pace, akin to my pre-*Tribune* days as a young police reporter for the City News Bureau. In my first week on the beat, hijackers broke into a boxcar sitting in a rail yard and hauled away 220 Scott deluxe floor model radios; they were caught three days later selling them at half the retail price out of a garage in an alley behind Cottage Grove Avenue.

Later that same week, a masked robber barged into the basement meeting room at a church on Archer Avenue one night with a shotgun and forced a dozen men–the church trustees–to stand along a wall. A second masked thug, brandishing two pistols, then took a bag containing $880 off a conference table and they both scrammed. The dough was earmarked for church maintenance and for charity, and the meeting had been called to dole it out. It smelled like an inside job to me, like maybe one of the trustees set it up and was going to get a three-way split with the hoodlums. Maybe that's my cynicism at work again, but in any case, the swag was never recovered.

Both of these were pretty good stories, and before the

war, they would have gotten nice play, maybe even at the bottom of Page 1. But both ended up as three-paragraph items somewhere back around Page 19. War news now dominated the paper, which was of course as it should be, but it was nonetheless frustrating to know that it was damn near impossible for a police reporter, particularly one out in the field, to get a story on the front page.

Because I was at the Hyde Park station most days, I started making it a habit to grab lunch at the University Tavern, which served good hamburgers and club sandwiches and a passable beef stew. I usually parked at the bar to eat, but always had coffee rather than beer. I was, after all, at work. I continued to try keeping my alcohol intake down; drink had messed up my life enough.

Chester the bartender, who began referring to me as "Mr. Java" because of my coffee consumption, became somewhat more friendly than on my first visits, although far from chummy. After he learned that I was a *Trib* reporter–I made no effort to hide the fact–he asked almost every day if there were any developments on the Bergman murder.

"None yet," was my usual and truthful reply. I had asked MacAfee to stay on top of the case with Fergus Fahey and report any breakthroughs to me. So far there were none.

"The professor, he was a good man," Chester

grunted, running a thick hand through his close-cropped salt-and-pepper hair. "Wouldn't a hurt a flea. Strange what happened."

"Indeed. Do you have any theories?"

He shook his head. "No idea. Other than chatting with folks at the bar–usually people he didn't know–he didn't seem to have a lot of close friends. Or if he did, they never came around here. Oh, once in a while, one of the other profs from his department would drop by and they'd exchange a few words. Hey, speaking of the devil…one of them just came in." He pointed across the big, dark room, where Nate Lazar was stepping in the door and shucking off his overcoat.

He waved to me and came over. "Mr…Malek, right? I didn't expect to see you here," he said, shaking hands.

"I'm stationed in this part of town for awhile," I told him. "And I often have lunch here."

"Ah, are you here because of…Arthur?"

"Not really. Just swapped places with another reporter for awhile."

"Really? Well, welcome to the neighborhood," Lazar said heartily. "I drop in occasionally for lunch, especially when I'm in the mood for a really good hamburger, and they're excellent here, as you have no doubt found. Also, from time to time I feel the need to escape the campus. It can tend to be a bit on the stifling side sometimes."

"Well, pull up a stool, unless you prefer more elegant seating," I said.

"Stool's fine, although I'm usually at a table. And I just want lunch, no cocktail."

"Same as me," I told him, holding up my coffee cup. "Have you met Chester?"

"Seen you, but never been introduced. Name's Lazar, Nate Lazar," he said, reaching across the mahogany surface and pumping the bartender's broad paw.

Chester mumbled something that sounded vaguely like "nice to meet you" and handed him a menu. "Just a hamburger plate for me," Lazar said. "Medium rare…and coffee, black."

"With us here drinking coffee, Chester is going to wonder if his long row of stools is gradually turning into a teetotalers' hangout," I said as the bartender lumbered off to place the order. "What's the talk around the campus now about the Bergman killing?"

"Ever the reporter, eh? Well, there's been all sorts of speculation, of course, some of it pretty wild. One theory–I've heard this from a couple of people in the department–is that Arthur was a German spy who'd infiltrated the department and the so-called nuclear project that a lot of us think is being conducted in the Metallurgy Lab. The spy stuff is total hogwash, of course. Arthur was a patriot if there ever was one. He was from Minnesota, studied at MIT, had never even been to Germany as far as I know. And he volunteered for military service a month after Pearl Harbor, which is more than I can say for any of his colleagues in the Physics

116

Department, present company included. He was turned down because of his eyesight. Without those Coke-bottle-bottom lenses, he couldn't see five feet in front of him."

"Okay, let's scratch the spy theory," I said. "What's some of the other speculation you've heard?"

"That he was keeping a hoard of money in his apartment, hundreds of thousands of dollars left to him by his mother, who died last year. But that's ridiculous, too. Arthur was nothing if not practical," Lazar said as Chester put a cup of coffee in front of him. "If he *had* been left a large sum by Mama up in Minneapolis, which I seriously doubt, he would have banked it where he could get the highest rate of interest."

"Anything else–maybe an angry husband? Or...some other man?"

Lazar frowned. "I'll take the latter question first," he said in a disapproving tone. "If you're suggesting that Arthur was a homosexual, you're completely off base. He had a lustful appreciation for women, attractive women. He married two of them, one of whom was at the funeral. You may have seen her. And I'm told that both of his marriages broke up because of his roving eye and his roving habits."

"Yes, I noticed the ex-wife at the funeral. A real knockout. I would have figured having somebody like that at home would keep a guy from straying."

"You'd think so, all right. And Irene is more than

beautiful, she's a very bright, extremely personable woman. Arthur was crazy to cheat on her. She has two degrees in English from Chicago and she's had a historical novel published, plus I believe she's working on another book now. And she's a physical fitness enthusiast– belongs to a group called Sokol."

"Yes, I know of the organization. The word is Czech for 'falcon.'"

"That figures–she's of Bohemian extraction, as I suppose you are with your name."

"Yes, I am."

"When they were still married, Vera–that's my wife– Vera and I would get together with them occasionally for dinner or bridge. We both liked Irene a lot. Which brings me back to your first question. To my knowledge, Arthur was only interested in single women. We were having lunch a couple of years ago, and in a rare moment of candor, he mentioned something about never wanting to get into a situation with a married woman. There was one–a married one, that is–at a physics conference who made some obvious overtures to him, and he ran away from that situation like it was a plague. And I know the woman in question–she's beautiful."

"Okay, I'll concede the point," I told him. "But if he was supposed to be such a ladies' man, why did he hang around this place so much?"

"That's been a relatively recent development," Lazar said as Chester delivered his hamburger. "His divorce from Irene seemed to hit him pretty hard, although he'd behaved disgracefully to her. Apparently, he felt she'd never pack her bags and walk out. He figured wrong. After their split, he fell into a depression, and from what I've observed, mostly at a distance, I don't think he ever fully came out of it. The increased drinking–most of it right here–was probably a manifestation of that depression."

"Do you know any more about what his role might have been in, well…weapons development?"

Lazar shook his head. "The lid's really screwed on tight. Something is definitely happening over at the Met Lab, no question, and it's a fair bet that Arthur was involved in it. He was easily the most brilliant among us, and he wasn't teaching much this term, as I think you know. Several of us in the department asked him what he was working on with all that free time that he had. Now that I look back on it, his answers were always vague, or maybe evasive is a more accurate term."

"Didn't that set off warning bells in your head?"

He took the last bite of his hamburger and swiveled on the stool to face me, wiping crumbs from his mustache. "Mr. Malek, we are all terribly busy with our own teaching and research and writing and families and heaven knows what else. I, for one, really didn't spend a lot of time wondering about what Arthur was up to, and I suspect none of his other colleagues in the Physics Department did, either. It's only now that we're trying to

119

recall details, things that he said that might throw some light on what's happened."

"Well, if the cops have gotten anywhere, they aren't talking about it, at least not to the press."

"With all the security and government restrictions around here these days–you've seen uniformed soldiers standing guard in front of boarded-up campus buildings– the police themselves may be stymied by the hush-hush nature of this place. Sorry to say, but in the grand scheme of things, Arthur Bergman's death, tragic as it is, pales in significance to what's being done to knock off the Axis."

"Agreed. Except that maybe his death had something to do with what's being done to knock off the Axis."

Lazar nodded somberly and contemplated his empty coffee cup. "Well, I've got to head back to work, Mr. Malek." He reached for his check, but I snatched it. "This is on me."

I got a grin out of him. "All right, on one condition," he said. "That I buy you lunch over on the campus, at Hutchinson Commons. I don't want to be in your debt. You've bought drinks once, and now lunch. Next one is my treat. And I'll see if I can round up some of the others that you met at the funeral. Who knows–maybe something will come to light. How about Friday at noon?"

"You've got yourself a deal," I said. "One more thing: Do you know where I can reach Irene–the former Mrs. Bergman?"

"I'm not sure what you'll be able to learn from her that will help, but you're the one doing the investigating. As far as I know, Irene's still in the Powhatan, where she and Arthur lived before their divorce. It's one of those tall apartment buildings with Indian names that cluster together along the shoreline on Chicago Beach at around 50th Street. You can walk there in about fifteen minutes. I assume she's in the phone book under 'Bergman.' I'm pretty sure she kept the name after the split."

I thanked Lazar, who left. I then settled the bill with Chester and headed back to the Hyde Park precinct station to phone one Irene Bergman.

Chapter 13

Back at the station house, I phoned the other precincts on my beat. The only thing I came up with was a currency exchange heist in the Grand Crossing district that netted a pistol-toting robber $213 and change. I called it in to the *Trib*, where an ever-bored rewrite man, Chick Henson, took down the information with his usual lack of enthusiasm. After hanging up, I made it three-to-one that the item would never run. For the record, it didn't.

Next, I paged through the new phone book and found a number for 'Bergman, I.' at 4950 S. Chicago Beach Drive. She answered on the third ring.

"Mrs. Bergman?" I asked.

Her "yes" sounded guarded.

"My name is Steve Malek. I'm a reporter for the *Tribune* and would like to talk to you about your ex-husband."

A pause. "What is it you wish to know?" The tone was somewhere between icy and standoffish.

"I realize this is a painful subject, but if you could spare a half hour or so, I'd like to stop by. Or we could meet for coffee somewhere in the neighborhood. I'm just a few minutes away. I'm calling from the Hyde Park police station over on Lake Park Avenue."

Another pause, this one longer. "I really don't know how I can help you. You probably are aware that we were divorced."

"Yes, I am. And I don't mean to be presumptuous, but I'm hoping you might have some insights."

"What kind of insights?"

"On his life, his work, the people he knew."

"Is this for some sort of feature story?"

"I honestly won't know until we've talked. But I can assure you that I'm not looking to do a sensational article."

"Well, I shouldn't think so; that's hardly the *Tribune's* style, is it?" I sensed a slight thaw in her voice.

"No, it's not. And I'm no Johnny-come-lately. I've been with the paper for more than ten years."

The next pause was the longest of all. "All right," she said with a sigh. "Why don't you come over here? As I guess you know, I'm at the Powhatan. The doorman will send you up to my place on the tenth floor."

"I'll be there in twenty minutes."

I had never seen anything like the Powhatan Apartments. The ornate double doors at the entrance had metal grilles in the shapes of American Indians. The oval foyer was a sort of gold color, and mosaics around the ceiling showed exotic colored images of women and animals and flowers. I was probably gawking like a rube on his first trip to the big city when a deep voice asked, "Can I help you, sir?"

The uniformed doorman sat at a desk against one wall. "Quite a sight, isn't it?" he said. "I can always tell the first-time visitors to this building. Who are you here to see?"

"Mrs. Bergman."

"Your name?"

"Steve Malek. She's expecting me."

He picked up his phone and dialed a number, saying something into the receiver that I couldn't hear and then nodding in my direction. "The elevator's right over there, sir. Marcus, take this gentleman up to Ten."

The elevator's interior looked like a small foyer, with a streamlined ceiling fixture, vertical gold fluting on the walls, and a modernistic mirror that had a geometric pattern cut into the glass. "This is quite a deal," I said to Marcus, as we started upward. "All it needs is a sofa, an end table, and a reading lamp."

"Glad you like it, sir," he answered primly. "Going to see Mrs. Bergman, correct?"

"Correct, Marcus."

I felt I should tip him when he opened the doors at the tenth floor. I resisted the temptation, but did thank him–it seemed the thing to do in these elegant surroundings.

I rang the buzzer at her door and heard the clicking of heels from inside. The woman who opened the door was even lovelier than I remembered from the funeral. I'm not good with ages, particularly with women, but I put her at about thirty-five. She was close to my height, and I'm a fraction over six feet. Her hair, a shade too dark to be termed platinum, but solidly in the blonde spectrum, framed a face that would have been right at home on a motion picture screen. Bergman must have been out of his mind to walk away from this.

"Mr. Malek?" she said, arching one eyebrow. She wasn't smiling, but she wasn't frowning, either, which was a start.

"At your service," I responded, grinning and holding up my police press card, which had my mug shot on it.

"Oh, yes, I recognize you from the funeral. You were the only person there I couldn't identify. Come in, please," Irene Bergman said, stepping aside gracefully. She wore those satin lounging pajamas now all the rage, according to the fashion pages in the papers. If the apartment wasn't as ornate as the lobby downstairs, it seemed pretty close to it at first glance. I found myself in a sleek foyer complete with an inlaid tile floor, mirrors on three walls, and indirect ceiling lighting that cast a warm glow.

Two steps down was a white-carpeted living room larger than my entire apartment, with two sofas, a love seat, a half-dozen chairs, several floor lamps, a chrome-

and-mirrored bar in one corner, and three large windows looking out over the slate-gray lake.

"Beautiful place," I observed as she took my coat and hat. "And in a beautiful building, as well. I had no idea what was down this way."

"Aha," she said, clapping once and allowing herself a smile. "I believe I am in the presence of a North Sider. True?"

"Guilty as charged. I live on Clark, north of Belmont."

"Well, I am delighted to report that there is indeed life far south of Madison Street, Mr. Malek. You are now in one of the buildings of the so-called 'Indian Village.' Our neighboring towers also have the names of tribes: Algonquin, Chippewa, Narragansett. Can I get you coffee...or something stronger?"

"Nothing, thanks," I said, stepping into the room and pulling a reporters' notebook from my suit coat pocket. "I like the style of the building, and of your apartment. What would you call it?"

"Art Moderne is the term I hear most frequently from those who know more than I about such things. Please, sit down anywhere."

I dropped into a boxy beige chair that was surprisingly comfortable, while my hostess sat at right angles to me on a sofa, crossing one slender ankle over the other. "So, Mr. Malek, before you get started with your questions, let me answer one that you haven't asked but would like to."

"Oh? I can hardly wait."

She made a sweeping gesture with one arm. "You are wondering how I–or even Arthur and I together when we were married–could afford to live like this."

"I guess it might have been in the back of my mind."

"That's only natural. Mr. Malek, I'm fortunate to have come from a very enterprising family. My father came over here from Bohemia at the start of the century and founded an extremely successful home construction business–Vorchek Builders."

"Of course. I've seen yellow-and-green Vorchek trucks all over the city," I said.

"Yes, they're hard to miss. You could choose to call my father's achievements good timing on his part, given the housing boom that came along after the Armistice. But that would be overlooking the terribly hard work and long hours that he–and my mother–put into establishing and operating the company. While he was out building the houses–whole blocks of brick bungalows in some city neighborhoods and in suburbs like Berwyn and Elmhurst– she was at home tending to my brother and me and doing the bookkeeping until he could afford an office staff."

"I'm impressed."

"That wasn't my purpose," Irene Bergman said quietly. "I merely wanted you to know how things were with Arthur and me. Some friends of his, and some of mine, thought that he pursued me and married me for, well, for my...money. But the truth is that it was I who pursued him. Are you surprised?"

"I've been a newspaperman for a lot of years now. Very little surprises me."

"A very diplomatic answer indeed. I know that people have wondered what I saw in him, although almost no one came right out and asked. While he was hardly physically attractive, he was a brilliant man–brighter by far, I believe, than most of his contemporaries at the university. And he had a certain off-beat charm that I found quite appealing. I take it that you never met him?"

"Actually, I did, one night at the University Tavern not long ago. We were on adjoining stools at the bar."

She considered me with interest. "How is it that a North Sider happened to be down here in one of our watering holes when you've got all sorts of high-toned places up there along Rush Street?"

"I'm currently covering the South Side police precincts for the *Trib,* so I spend quite a bit of time down here," I replied evenly, skipping over the circumstances and the sequence of events that led me to this part of the city.

"I'm interested in your impression of Arthur," she said.

I laughed. "I came here with questions, and it's you who is interviewing me."

A slight rosiness colored her alabaster cheeks. "Oh, I'm sorry," she said as if she meant it.

"Please don't be. As to your husband–ex-husband–I found him somewhat cryptic and mysterious."

Now it was her turn to laugh. "That sounds like Arthur," she said. "He always enjoyed giving the impression that he knew more about almost any subject than he was letting on."

"Did he? Know more, I mean?"

She leaned forward. "I'm going to have a cigarette. Would you like one?"

"Sure," I said, reaching into my pocket. "Let me–"

"No, I've got some, if Chesterfields are all right with you," she said, offering me one from a silver case. "They're just fine," I answered, lighting both of ours with my Zippo.

"As to how much Arthur knew about goings-on at the university," Irene said, taking a long drag from her cigarette, "I was never really sure. He loved to play the man of mystery."

"The reason I'm asking is that he may have been working on some sort of super-secret war weapon. Do you know anything about that?"

She shook her head. "I've heard rumors, but only at places like cocktail parties, and then just very vague references from people who didn't sound like they knew what they were talking about. Arthur himself never alluded to a weapon in our conversations, but of course we were already separated at this time last year, which was even before Pearl Harbor. So if he was working on something big, it probably began after we parted ways. What exactly did he say to you?"

I gave her the gist of our conversation, including the "you don't know what I know" part and the "at the place where we surrendered, that's where we shall rise again" riddle.

She ground out her cigarette butt in a triangular crystal ash tray. "As I said before, that sounds like Arthur, dripping with intrigue. And as I also said before, he was a gifted man, dazzlingly brilliant in his field, as several of his colleagues told me. Never mind that he had a roving eye, particularly for nubile coeds, who seemed drawn to him–but that's another story. If any younger member of the Physics Department were asked to participate in the development of some kind of advanced weapon, I'm sure it would have been Arthur."

"Do you know of anybody who would want him dead?"

"The police asked me that, too, as you would expect," she said. "And I'll tell you exactly what I told them: My former husband was far from being gregarious and outwardly likeable, but to my knowledge, he didn't have any real enemies. Oh, I think there may have been some professional jealousy within the department from time to time, and it's possible that some colleagues may have resented Arthur because of grants he was given and trips he got to conferences, some of them overseas. There can be a lot of pettiness in the academic world."

"Anybody specific who intensely disliked him?"

"No one that I am aware of, although I know he wasn't particularly fond of some people in the department."

"Who?"

She frowned. "I don't like to sound like a gossip— there's enough of that on the campus."

"I never reveal my sources," I assured her.

"Well, there are a couple of professors, associate profs actually, whom Arthur didn't get along with. You might have met them at the funeral: Miles Overby and Theo Ward."

"Yes, I did spend a little time with them. What was the problem?"

Irene shrugged. "Arthur didn't think they were first-rate scientific minds and felt they tended to be somewhat lazy, especially Ward. And my sense from meeting them in social situations is that neither of them had any great fondness for Arthur, either. Having said that, I would not call them *enemies* of his. That's much too strong a word. And murder…" She waved the idea away with a manicured hand. "Unthinkable."

"What about one of the others that I met at the funeral—Edward Rickman?"

"I think he and Arthur had a mutual respect, even though they both were ambitious."

"And Lazar?"

"Nate is a real sweetheart," she said, "a dear. We

used to get together socially with him and his wife on occasion and had good times. He was Arthur's one true, loyal friend in the department. Please give him my best when you see him. Mr. Malek, if you're looking for reasons why Arthur was killed, I'm afraid I haven't been much help."

"Everything's helpful," I said, then shifted gears. "I understand from Lazar that you are an author."

"Of sorts. Before we get into that, would you think it terribly rude if I poured myself a scotch?"

"Not at all."

"Can I mix you one, too?" she asked, gliding over to the bar.

"Do you have beer?"

Irene reached into a refrigerated cabinet in the bar and came up with a Schlitz, which she poured into a tilted Pilsener glass.

"That's exactly the right amount of foam," I said as she handed me the glass.

"I learned that from my father, who always had me pour him his beer when I was a little girl," she said proudly, settling back into the sofa. "You asked if I'm an author. I've had one book published, a novel set in the British Isles at the time of Oliver Cromwell's rule. It got a couple of fairly good reviews, including in your *Tribune*"–she saluted me with her scotch on the rocks– "but it hasn't sold that well. My publisher is small, and on top of that, there's apparently not a big market right now

133

for stories set in 17th Century England. I'm working on a second novel, this one about a family in Maryland torn apart by divided loyalties during the Civil War. Don't expect this one to crash the best-seller lists either. But as you can see, I love history, even if it doesn't sell copies."

"Here's hoping book number two surprises you and takes the country by storm," I said, hoisting my glass to her. "Say, this is an interesting photo," I remarked, picking up a framed picture that was on the end table next to me. It was of a somewhat younger Irene in white shorts, white blouse, and tennis shoes posing with her arms spread as if caught in the middle of an exercise.

"Oh, I don't know why I still keep that out," Irene said with mock embarrassment. "It's a shot of me at a Sokol gathering a few years ago. Sokol is–"

"A Czech physical fitness and cultural organization," I interrupted. "Sokol is the Bohemian word for falcon."

"Well, aren't you the smart one," she said, tossing her head.

"I was in it for awhile growing up in Pilsen," I told her. "But then I discovered girls."

That got a laugh. "Of course–your name is Czech, I wasn't thinking," she said, finishing her scotch. "Well, I've stayed with it over the years. I like to keep in condition, and I find it's a good counterpoint to my writing, which is so sedentary. Some women take ballet lessons or play tennis or swim to stay in shape. For me, it's Sokol."

"It seems to be working," I observed.

"You are too kind, Mr. Malek. Can I get you another beer?"

"No thanks. I should go back to the Hyde Park station and try to justify my existence as a police reporter," I said, rising. "Again, I have to say that I'm really impressed with your place. I'm sure your ex-husband didn't live in anything approaching this style after the divorce, did he?"

"I suppose not," she said smoothly. "He was in some building over on Cornell, but I'm not very familiar with that area.

"I'm sorry that I wasn't much help with your story or your investigation or whatever you plan to do," she said in the foyer as she handed me my coat and hat. "Arthur's death just doesn't make any sense at all. Such a loss. Such a waste."

"Agreed. If I think of anything else to ask, may I call you?"

"Yes–absolutely. I'm here most days. Please feel free to stop by."

I told her I might just do that.

Chapter 14

The war constantly changed the way we lived. I had now been issued my first ration book for food. Gasoline rationing was set to start in December. Since I didn't own an automobile, that did not pose a hardship for me; however, the street cars, buses, elevated lines, and commuter trains were now always packed, as motorists gearing up for the rationing were leaving their vehicles at home.

On that Friday morning, my Illinois Central train south from the Loop was so crowded that I had to stand, even though we were running in the opposite direction from the rush hour traffic. I got to the Hyde Park precinct station a few minutes before nine, found out from Waldron that nothing worth reporting was going on there, and began calling the other station houses on my beat.

There wasn't much of interest until I talked to the desk sergeant at the Wentworth district, Cavanaugh, whom I had met on a visit to that precinct the week before.

"Ah, Malek, I believe I've got a good one for ye," he said in a brogue that I suspected he practiced at home every night. "Several people were waitin' for a northbound street car on State at 47th early this mornin' when this dip sneaks up behind them and tries to lift a wallet from a gent who was readin' his paper. A woman in the little crowd spots the pickpocket in the act and whacks him across the head with her purse. Two other ladies, and they weren't all that young, mind ye, join in, and start whackin' the fella, one of them with a damned umbrella. Soon he's down on the sidewalk, all huddled up, howlin' like a hoot owl and tryin' to protect his head with his hands as these ladies are whalin' away and kickin' him. Must have been quite a sight. Along about this time, one of our cruisers happens by and sees the fracas, and they haul the pathetic bloke in, bleedin' head and all. He's in our lockup now, name's Ferguson, Jack 'Nimble Fingers' Ferguson. Has a rap sheet for pickin' pockets that would like to strangle a horse. I've got the ladies' names if you want them, dear souls that they are. They're still here."

"Thank you, Sergeant," I said. "What you've told me is worth a visit to your esteemed establishment. Try to keep these fine ladies occupied until I get there." Twenty minutes later, I was in the dingy Wentworth station house, courtesy of a Checker cabbie who seemed to think red lights were only subtle suggestions to slow down.

I found the women at the station when I got there, relishing their role in nailing the luckless Mr. Ferguson. One of them, Maude Murray, a silver-haired grandmother wearing a black hat decorated with an artificial rose, told me she had had her purse lifted at a street car stop several years ago. "I've never forgotten that," she told me with emotion, balling her small hands into fists. "I vowed it would never happen to me again, or to anyone near me. What occurred today was clearly the work of the Lord. He wanted me there at that moment. And you may quote me in your newspaper."

Oh, I did. My story ended up getting good play on Page 6 the next day under a two-column, two-line headline: "Ladies Wield Purses to Foil Pickpocket." That was about the best one could expect from the South police beat.

I got back to Hyde Park a few minutes before noon and went directly to Hutchinson Commons on 57th Street to meet Nate Lazar for lunch. He was waiting for me at the entrance to the stately campus building.

"Perfect timing. Just got here myself," he said as we went inside and up a stairway.

"Quite the edifice," I said. "Looks like my impression of England, although I've never been there."

"That was the idea when old John D. Rockefeller himself ponied up the dough for this institution. Oxford on the Midway, or maybe Cambridge. Here we are," he said as we got to the top of the stairs. "And, just so you know, it's supposed to be bad luck to step on the seal."

Embedded into the tile floor in the hallway was the seal of the university, in bronze. Everyone skirted it.

"Even in a place of advanced learning, superstition lives, eh?"

"Absolutely," Lazar said. "I suspect there's more of that sort of thing here than many of us care to admit. Let's get in line. Remember, this is on me, so take whatever looks good to you."

The dining room was a long, cavernous hall two stories high, looking more like a cathedral than a cafeteria with its vaulted ceiling, Gothic ornamentation, stone fireplaces, and dark, paneled walls with paintings of university presidents and trustees. There must have been two hundred people in the big room–students, faculty, and probably other miscellaneous visitors like myself.

"The food isn't quite what it was before the war," Lazar said as we moved our trays along the line making selections, "but it's still decent. They have particularly good roasted chicken."

I opted for the chicken, with mashed potatoes and peas, and we camped at an unoccupied wooden table for four.

"Theo Ward might be joining us," Lazar said. "I told him you were coming, and, oh–there he is now." Lazar waved, and Ward picked his way through the mass of tables with his tray.

"This place gets more crowded by the day," Ward huffed as he settled in and began attacking his lunch. "Hello, Mr. Malek. Welcome to our campus madhouse. The original Bedlam couldn't have been this noisy."

"Now, Theo, it's simply hundreds of people engaged in animated conversation while they eat," Lazar chided. "You wouldn't want to stifle all that enthusiasm, much of it from students and likely brought on by the classroom stimulation provided by professors like yourself."

Ward grunted between bites. "Well, all I can say is–wait a minute, isn't that the great man himself, coming this way?" He gestured toward a stocky, balding gent in a three-piece suit who was carrying a tray of empty plates and headed in our direction.

Lazar nodded. "Enrico Fermi."

"Deigning to eat with us commoners," Ward said. "Thought that he'd be across the street at the Quadrangle Club with all the swells. Well, I've always wanted to meet him. Why not now?"

As Fermi got closer, Ward stood. "Dr. Fermi, I'm Theo Ward, an associate professor in the Physics Department."

"Uh, hello, nice to meet you," Fermi said in an accented voice. "I would shake your hand but..." He nodded to the tray he was holding.

"That's all right, Doctor. I'd like you to meet a colleague in the department, Nate Lazar. And this is a friend of ours, Steven Malek."

"A pleasure," Fermi said, looking at us in turn, his blue-gray eyes friendly.

"Doctor Fermi, it is our pleasure to have you on the campus," Ward said smoothly. "It has been widely known that you are here, of course, but many of us have wondered what type of projects you are working on."

Fermi looked uncomfortable, then shrugged. "Your people at this great university have very kindly invited me here to help them with some research in the Metallurgy Laboratory," he said. "I am very flattered to be asked to this fine institution, of course. I only hope that I will be able to contribute something to their work in metals. Now if you will kindly excuse me, I am late for a conference. It was good to meet you all." He bowed and went to put his tray on the return shelf.

"Now there was a man reading from a script if I ever saw one," Ward said with a scowl.

"What did you expect him to say, Theo?" Lazar asked. "That he's working on some kind of super-secret weapon?"

"It was worth a try. He has to know that people are curious, and suspicious, about what he's doing in these hallowed and ivy-covered halls of ours."

"Of course he knows," Lazar said. "Which is why he has undoubtedly memorized the speech he just gave you."

Ward turned to me. "You'll notice that I didn't give your profession away and send him running, Mister Newspaperman. What's your opinion?"

"Hard to tell. I'd have to spend more time with him, which seems unlikely. Appears to be a pleasant enough joe."

That got a chuckle out of Ward. "What a prosaic way

to describe a Nobel Laureate."

"Sorry, but that's all I have to go on," I responded, trying to hide my irritation.

"Don't let Theo get under your skin," Lazar said calmly. "Just as Fermi happened by, I was about to ask if you had heard anything more about Arthur's murder."

"Not a damned thing," I answered truthfully. "The guy who's been filling in for me at Headquarters checks with the Chief of Detectives every day, and there haven't been any breaks in the case."

"Huh! And just how hard have they been trying?" Ward snapped.

"Tough to say. It's possible the Feds have whistled them off."

"So you think they–the Feds–feel that what happened to Arthur has to do with national security?" Lazar asked.

"It wouldn't surprise me."

"Well, I think the police ought to take a long, hard look at Bergman's former wife if they haven't already," Ward said.

Lazar slammed his fork down on the table. "Theo, what are you talking about? That is a terrible thing to say!"

"Dammit, you were beguiled by that woman from the start, Nate. I'll grant you that she's easy to look at, but beneath that soft, feminine exterior is one tough, hard, calculating woman. Why she ever got interested in Arthur will always be a mystery to me, but she did. And then, two or three years into their marriage, when he started playing games with some of the female students, she became enraged. She couldn't believe any man would do that to her. Do you deny it?"

Lazar fidgeted in his chair. "No…but I can't imagine Irene doing something violent."

"Why not?" Ward demanded. "She's proud, she's strong, and she's a physical-fitness fanatic. Arthur used to brag about how she took part in those mass exercises that Bohemian group held, what's its name?"

"Sokol," I put in.

Ward nodded vigorously, causing his double chins to quiver. "Yes, that's it. Anyway, she could easily have dispatched her husband; she's a lot stronger than he ever was."

Lazar looked down, holding his head in his hand. "Theo, Theo, this never could have happened. She's not that kind of–"

Ward cut him off. "Mr. Malek, have the police questioned Irene Bergman?"

"I believe they have, but that would be expected."

"And?"

"They haven't charged her with anything, or we'd know about it."

"They're probably still gathering evidence," Ward snorted.

Lazar sighed. "Theo, what has gotten into you? Why this animosity toward Irene?"

"I realize Arthur was cheating on her, Nate, but I'll bet you didn't know she was cheating on him, too–and I think that was even before he started fooling around."

"Nonsense!"

"Believe it," Ward said grimly. "I never said anything about this before, but a couple of years ago, when Arthur was at a physics conference out East, in Boston I think, I happened to be walking along Dorchester north of the campus one night, and Irene came out of an apartment building on the arm of Dieter Schmid. The building happens to be the one Schmid lives in. They didn't see me; I was on the other side of the street."

"Who's Schmid?" I asked.

"Another professor in the Physics Department," Lazar said.

"German?"

"Swiss. He's been here for several years," Ward put in.

"It could have been very innocent," Lazar insisted.

"I grant you that it could have been," Ward said nodding, "except for their embrace and long kiss at the bottom of the stairs before they went off in opposite directions. And that kiss was not the type a brother gives to a sister."

"I'm not sure I see the point of all this," I told Ward as Lazar wore an increasingly disconsolate expression. "These are adults having affairs. For good or ill, this sort of thing happens to all sorts of people, all the time. How does it point to Bergman's killing?"

"I don't believe Irene ever really cared for Arthur," Ward said. "She may have been impressed by his intellect, but she couldn't have loved him."

"Why not?"

"Arthur was a hard man to like, let alone love," Ward said. "I've always been amazed that he had so much, shall we say…success with female students."

"Now this is what I call a truly motley crew–of course excluding you from that description, Mr. Malek," Miles Overby boomed as he approached our table. "If I were to make a wild guess, I would say the subject of discussion here is Arthur's demise."

"And you would of course be correct, Miles," Ward said. "Join us."

"Just for a minute or two. I was dining over in the far corner, with a former student now at Cal Tech, and I've got to get back to the office for some student conferences."

Ward nodded. "I was just talking about Irene."

"Ah, the not-so-grieving ex-wife?" Overby said, folding his lanky frame into the fourth chair at the table.

Lazar made a face. "Miles, don't tell me you have got it in for her, too."

"Not at all," Overby said, turning a hand over. "It's just that I never saw much warmth between them. It seemed like a strange marriage from the start."

"Well, your colleague here thinks she might have

bumped him off," I said, gesturing in Ward's direction.

"Really?" Overby's angular face registered surprise. "How did you come up with that?"

"Mr. Malek overstates my comment. I did not make an outright accusation," Ward protested. "I only suggested it as a possibility." He then proceeded to repeat his story about seeing the extended embrace between Irene and Dieter Schmid.

"Who'd have thought Dieter had it in him?" Overby said with a chuckle. "I always felt his only passion was his work. That is, if he's capable of any passion at all."

"It would appear from what Mr. Ward saw that he is," I remarked.

"You're all gossiping like a bunch of old crones!" Lazar fumed. "Whatever may have happened between Irene and Schmid hardly suggests her as a murderer."

"I have to agree," I put in. "Tell me about this Schmid fellow."

"Brilliant by all accounts," Overby said, "although very taciturn, to the extent that it's hard to get complete sentences out of him. Seems unfriendly on the surface, but I think it's more a case that he's shy and not strong in the social skills."

"Except with Irene," Ward said.

"Is he part of this Metallurgy Lab business?" I asked.

Lazar nodded. "I think so, although as we've said, that operation is so secretive that it's not always easy to determine."

Ward snorted. "You'd keep it a secret, too, if you were working on something so lethal it could reduce the entire city of Chicago to a pile of rubble."

"There you go again, Theo," Lazar said. "Remember, we have no hard-and-fast evidence about what's going on over there."

"No, but we have a pretty damned good idea, you have to admit that," Ward fired back.

"Was Schmid at the Bergman funeral?" I asked, trying to steer the subject back to the murder.

"No," Overby said. "They weren't particularly close."

"Does that mean there was animosity between them?" I asked.

"I'm not aware of any, are either of you?" Overby posed. Lazar and Ward shook their heads.

"Arthur and Schmid didn't travel in the same circles–unless you were to count Irene," Ward said sardonically. "And if I were to guess, I'd say that Arthur never knew he was being cuckolded by a colleague."

"I'd agree," Overby said. "And if anybody wants my vote, it's that Irene did not kill Arthur, although she probably is strong enough to do the job."

"All right," Ward sighed, throwing his hands up. "To make everybody happy, I hereby stipulate that Irene is not the culprit. Are there other nominations?"

We all looked at one another blankly. "There being none, I move we adjourn," Lazar said. "Mr. Malek, thank you so much for joining me today."

"Thank you for hosting me," I told him. "I wouldn't have missed it. And I assure you gentlemen that if and when I hear anything, you'll be the first to know, after my editors."

Chapter 15

Holidays didn't have the same meaning for me that they once did. My parents were gone now, Dad having died in August of '39 and Mom just over a year later. And of course Peter spent most of the red-letter calendar days with Norma and Martin Baer, although he and I usually had our own delayed celebrations together a few days after the fact.

So it should have been no surprise that Thanksgiving snuck up on me again. Last year, I had eaten alone in my apartment–canned ham, not turkey. And this year I hadn't even given the November holiday a thought until the Sunday preceding it when I saw the restaurant ads in the *Tribune* for special Thanksgiving dinners.

The next morning, I looked up an Oak Park number in my address book that I hadn't called in more than four years and used the police phone in the Hyde Park precinct station. Catherine Reed answered on the second ring.

"Hi, it's Steve Malek. Glad I caught you at home. Thought you might be at the library today."

"Oh…hello, Steve. No, I'm still working three days a week until January, when I go to full time."

"Good. I was wondering if you'd like to have Thanksgiving dinner with me. We could go to some restaurant out in Oak Park or Forest Park...I'm sure a few of them will be open."

The pause at the other end lasted at least fifteen seconds, although it seemed longer. "Well...I had just planned to eat at home and–Steve, I have an idea: Why don't you come over here on Thursday?"

"I wasn't angling for an invitation," I said, probably sounding sheepish.

"I didn't think you were," Catherine said. "I can't claim to be a gourmet cook, but I already have the food for the dinner, and it's much more than enough for two. If you come, it will save me from having to eat leftovers for a week. I've already got a small turkey. It may be the last time I'll buy one for several years, what with all the food shortages and rationing that we're told are coming. And I'm also having dressing, along with sweet potatoes and cranberry sauce, and of course pumpkin pie."

"You have just sold me. What can I bring?"

"Just yourself. And some of those wonderful newspaper stories like the ones you told here at dinner with Daddy those times."

"I'll search my memory for some lively tales of life on the boulevards and byways of the city."

Noon on Thanksgiving found me aboard a Lake Street Elevated train rattling and swaying its way west from the Loop to the stately and proper village of Oak Park. I was toting a box of Fannie May chocolates and a bouquet of mums, and reading the final edition of the *Chicago Sun*. As the train neared its destination, it surprised me to find that I was nervous.

In spite of those four-plus years since my last visit, I had no trouble finding the solid two-story stucco house that lay a few blocks south of the Ridgeland Avenue El station. It looked exactly as it did when I had last visited Steel Trap Bascomb to plumb the blurred depths of his fading memory in my search for the murderer of a would-be Chicago mayor.

Catherine swung open the door just as my finger was poised at the buzzer. "I was keeping an eye out for you," she said. "It's too chilly to stand outside any longer than absolutely necessary."

"Actually, it's not bad for this time of year," I said, "but inside is better." Smiling, I stepped in and presented her with the flowers and candy.

"The mums I accept without reservation," she said, giving me a curtsy. "I absolutely insist that you help me consume the chocolates, however."

"Duly noted. And Catherine, I really like the aromas that are wafting in this direction," I said, putting a hand lightly on her shoulder.

"Here's hoping everything tastes as good as it smells," she said with a smile, as she hung my coat and hat on a rack inside the door. "I thought we could have some hot cider in the living room before eating."

"Lead me to it. How are you getting along, Catherine?" I asked, as we moved into the living room. I sat on the sofa and she went to the kitchen to get the cider.

"I'm doing all right," she said evenly, while serving the steaming cider in cups and then sliding into a chair across from me. "The house seems empty, though, which is only natural. It's funny—one of the things I miss most is the sound of that radio in the sitting room. Daddy had his favorite programs every night of the week."

"I remember 'Fibber McGee and Molly' from when I was here."

"Oh, yes! He never missed it. And when Fibber opened that closet and everything came clattering out, he would always slap his knee and laugh, no matter how many times he heard it. In fact, in his last years, he insisted that I buy Johnson's Wax products. He was afraid that if the show lost its sponsor, it would go off the air!"

"Talk about loyalty," I said with a grin.

"Yes. And he loved Jack Benny, too, particularly the way he joked about being thirty-nine forever. Just a few weeks ago, he surprised me by saying, 'Honey, in less than two years, I'll be exactly twice Benny's age.' Steve, this was the same man who didn't even know who I was an hour later."

"It had to be terribly rough for you," I said, reaching over and covering her hand with mine.

"The most frustrating part was that on any given day,

he could either be lucid or unresponsive. As I told you at the funeral home, a few weeks back he started wandering away from the house."

I nodded in sympathy. "Did he seem to be in a lot of pain?"

"If he was, he never showed it. And his appetite was good almost to the end."

"I remember that appetite, all right. Did you get all the clippings about him from the newspapers?"

"Just the one in the *Tribune*."

"I can get you those that ran in all the other papers. Our office keeps copies of every one of the dailies for a couple of months or more."

"That would be wonderful. I was wishing at the time that I had bought the other papers, but I was so busy with the funeral arrangements. I'd like to put all the write-ups about him into a scrapbook. Even though the family line will end with me, I want to leave a tangible record of his accomplishments. Someday, I'll probably give the scrapbook to the local historical society. After all, he lived in Oak Park for at least forty years, which practically makes him an old settler."

"Good idea, Catherine. I'd like to get you quotes from some of the old-timers who remember your father. I recall a *Daily News* police reporter, long dead now, talking to me years ago about him. As near as I can remember, these were his words: 'Steel Trap Bascomb had the sharpest mind of any newspaperman I ever met.

He could remember the first and last name–and the middle initial–of the patrolman who broke up a crap game in a garage fifteen years earlier. And he could remember the address of the game, as well as the number of guys in it, the color of the paint on the garage, and the amount of money on the table. Now there was a reporter.'"

Catherine had begun to tear up at this, so to break any tension, I said that I, in contrast, would have forgotten all the facts about a similar story a half hour after I'd phoned it in to a rewrite man.

"I don't believe that, not for a moment," she said as we moved into the dining room. "I suspect you've got a memory every bit as good as Daddy's was."

"Don't I wish. I've got a few editors up in Tribune Tower who would set you straight about that."

We sat down to eat and Catherine bowed her head and said a short prayer that closed with words about her father being "in a better place now."

"Steve, how is your son–Peter, isn't it? He must be in high school by now."

"You've got a good memory," I told her as I loaded my plate up with turkey, dressing, sweet potatoes, and cranberry sauce. "He's a sophomore at Lake View High, a reserve on the junior varsity football team, and gets good grades. Also, he's on a committee that's organizing scrap and newspaper drives for the war effort."

"You taught him well."

"Or Norma did."

"Do you see him often?"

"Almost every weekend. He's in an apartment over on the Drive. Norma remarried–fellow named Martin Baer, and Peter lives with them."

"Is that…all right with you?"

"I don't have a lot of choice in the matter. Norma got custody. But to be fair, Baer's a decent enough sort. He runs a men's store over at the Lincoln-Belmont-Ashland intersection that apparently does quite well. Among other things, Peter gets to go to Florida with them during Christmas vacation every year, which is more than I can do for him."

"But I'm sure you make up for it in other ways."

"I try to, as well as I can on a *Tribune* reporter's less-than-princely salary. We went to the Bears-Packers game just the other day."

"Speaking of the *Tribune*, how is your work going?" she asked. "Fill me in."

I gave her a brief rundown on my temporary shift to the South Side police beat and all the facets of Bergman's killing, including the speculation about a secret weapon being developed. I also told her about finding Bergman's body.

"That must have been awful."

"It was no picnic. Even though I've been a police reporter for more years than I care to think about and have seen a few murder victims, most of my experience with murder has been second-hand, and I would prefer to keep it that way."

"What do you think about this secret weapon talk?"

I shrugged. "I'm out of my depth there. I have no idea what might be going on, and if I did know, I'm sure I wouldn't understand it. Even those professors I mentioned, the ones who were colleagues of Bergman's, don't agree with each other on what's going on in that Metallurgy Laboratory, except that they all seem to think it's a cover for something that has nothing to do with metallurgy."

She set her fork down carefully on her plate and fixed me with guileless brown eyes. "Please be careful, Steve Malek."

"I'm always careful."

"So you say. I see someone who has a reckless side."

"I like to think of my style as aggressive and enterprising," I responded with a grin.

She kept those brown eyes fastened on me, which I found a little unnerving, although now she allowed herself a slight smile. "Call it what you like, but I still say, 'Be careful.'"

"I promise I will be. By the way, this meal has been wonderful."

"Don't change the subject; there's still dessert to come. Pumpkin pie a la mode," Catherine said. "Unless of course you are too full."

"Too full? Not a chance. Bring on that next course."

We ate the pumpkin pie and ice cream in silence, and

then Catherine poured coffee.

"This has been a wonderful dinner," I proclaimed, rubbing my stomach.

"I detect flattery," Catherine said, clearing the plates from the table. "I suppose you want more coffee?"

"I suppose I do. Is there a charge here for a second cup?"

"Normally," she said, not missing a beat, "but we waive that on Thanksgiving Day."

"Which is why this is such a wonderful a place to dine," I responded, holding my cup high in a salute.

"You're welcome to come back," Catherine said quietly.

"On one condition."

"Yes?"

"That before I come back, our next meal together is on me, and in a restaurant, either out here somewhere or downtown. Do you get to the city often?"

She shook her head. "Not for a long time, not with Daddy being, well…"

"Oh, of course. Do you think I might be able to lure you east across Austin Boulevard and into Chicago to dine at one of the cosmopolitan city's culinary palaces?"

She smiled but looked down. "Well, I believe I might consider the invitation."

I nodded. "That's a start. Catherine, the weather is mild for late November, in fact damn near balmy. How about a stroll to work off this wonderful meal?"

"Okay…sure." She undoubtedly remembered our last walk in this neighborhood, and so did I, which is why I suggested that we repeat it. Sometimes the way to erase a memory is to relive the experience, or so I told myself.

Catherine took my arm–a good sign–as we stepped out onto the empty sidewalk. We passed many houses where Thanksgiving feasts were surely taking place at this very moment. We had gone a couple of blocks when she gave my arm a tug and stopped on the sidewalk, facing me.

"I'm curious, Steve. What made you call me after all this time?"

"Well…"

"I think I know. After Daddy died, a little bit of pity, perhaps?"

"That's not true. When I saw you at the funeral parlor, I realized it would be nice to get together again."

"But why not four years ago?"

"Catherine, I was going through a confusing period then. My marriage had–"

She squeezed my arm. "No need to go on, Steve. I have no business questioning you. I'm sorry."

"Don't be. And please don't misunderstand what I'm about to say: I'm not happy that your father is gone, but I'm glad that it was the event that brought me back to Oak Park."

"I am too, Steve."

"Good. Now, unlike the last time you and I were

walking these very streets, I am going to escort you home." I got no argument.

Chapter 16

The Monday morning after Thanksgiving, the entire nation focused on one grim event: the horrific fire at the Cocoanut Grove nightclub in Boston over the weekend, which killed nearly 500 in the overcrowded building. Stampeding patrons had been stacked up at revolving doors in the rush to escape, and the cowboy film actor Buck Evans was among the dead. For one day, at least, the war got edged out as the lead story on Page 1 of papers across the country.

At noon, after an uneventful morning at the Hyde Park precinct and throughout the whole of the South Side, I was at the University Tavern bar, ordering lunch, drinking coffee, and reading newspaper accounts of the fire when Edward Rickman slid onto the stool next to me. "Mind if I join you?" he asked, tugging at the knot of his silk tie.

"Not at all. I didn't know you ate here."

"From time to time. I find it a refreshing change of scenery from the campus dining spots, where all the talk is thinly veiled faculty gossip–well, actually not always so thinly veiled. Terrible story, isn't it?" he said, gesturing to the Cocoanut Grove headline on the early edition of the *Daily News* that I had spread out on the bar.

"Awful. All those people partying, having fun after a college football game, and then..."

Rickman nodded solemnly. "Who lives and who dies seems so arbitrary, so random, even capricious. And it doesn't always have to do with your station in life. Most of the people in that club were probably from the upper crust, or at least the upper end of the middle crust. College students from good, solid families, successful alumni, community leaders."

"Live every day as though it's your last," I mused.

"Sorry to come in here and be so morbid," Rickman said. "Have you ordered lunch?"

"My usual, the hamburger plate. It's on the way."

"Can't go wrong with that. Chester, I'll have the same thing as this gentleman, including coffee," he called out to the burly barkeep, who turned to place the order with the kitchen. "Anything new on Arthur's death?"

"Not that I've heard. Do you have any fresh theories yourself?"

"Afraid I haven't."

"I assume you know Dieter Schmid."

"Yes, although not very well. Why do you ask?"

"It's a little piece of what you referred to a minute ago as 'faculty gossip.' Seems that he may have been involved with Bergman's wife."

Rickman looked surprised. "Really? I'm curious as

to the source of your information."

"Your colleague Mr. Ward says he saw them together in what might best be described as a compromising situation."

"What does that mean? Was Theo peeking into a bedroom window with binoculars?"

I laughed as Chester delivered my hamburger plate and a coffee refill. "No, one night he saw them on the street, embracing for an extended period."

"Well, she's a damned attractive woman, and divorced. If I weren't happily married myself, I would certainly be knocking on her door with flowers and candy in hand."

"She wasn't divorced a couple of years ago, when the aforesaid embrace took place."

"Hmm. I never heard Theo say anything about this."

"I was having lunch with Lazar a few days back at Hutchinson Commons and Ward stopped by and told us about it. Said he'd never mentioned it to anyone before. Overby dropped over for a minute, too. Anyway, Ward suggested that the former Mrs. Bergman might be a suspect."

"Irene? Ridiculous!"

"That seemed to be the majority opinion at the table as well."

"I should think so," Rickman huffed. "Talk about reaching."

"Well, in fairness to Mr. Ward, he backed down on

his assertion after the others jumped all over him."

"Good for them. Ah, here's my lunch. Thank you, Chester. How are things going in the Pacific?"

"All right, so far," the bartender muttered, nodding curtly.

"His son Len is a seaman on a destroyer," Rickman said sotto voce as Chester ambled toward the other end of the long bar. "I saw in the paper that we lost yet another destroyer in the Solomon Islands, and I was afraid something might have happened to Len. Chester doesn't talk a lot, but I know he's worried sick. The kid just missed catching it at Pearl Harbor. He was a crew member, a seaman, on one of the destroyers that got sunk, the *U.S.S. Downes,* but he was ashore in Honolulu at the time."

"Maybe that's why the barkeep is so dour all the time, although he has warmed to me slightly–very slightly. Or at least he's gotten used to my coming in here with some regularity."

"There have to be thousands like him all over the country, worried that every phone call or every mail delivery is going to bring dire news."

"True. Tell me more about this guy Schmid. He sounds like a German to me, although I understand he's Swiss."

Rickman chuckled. "Funny you should mention that, and in the U.T. of all places. He drops by on occasion for a drink, as I do, but we rarely sit together. As I said before, I don't know him all that well. I have nothing against him, mind you, but he's very reserved, generally keeps to himself.

"Anyway, just a few weeks ago, he came in here one night alone, nodded at me, and sat several stools away. A few minutes later, a chemistry professor, a hail-fellow type named Carver, sees Schmid and greets him in his booming voice, saying something like 'Well, if it isn't our house German, Herr Dieter Schmid. Zig heil!' Schmid looked like he wanted to crawl under a table."

"Doesn't sound like a particularly funny thing to say, especially not in these times."

"No," Rickman said, "but that's Carver. Knowing him, he meant no harm, but I think he'd had a few drinks before he got here. Anyway, I doubt if Schmid's been back since, although I'm not here often enough to know myself."

"Has anybody ever seriously suggested that he might be a German spy?"

"Not at all," Rickman said, waving the suggestion away with a hand. "He's been here for years, and he's a highly regarded physicist. And as I understand it, he's definitely Swiss, not German."

"Is he one of those who are working in the Metallurgy Lab?"

"I…think so. Like Bergman, he hasn't been teaching this term, which might suggest a 'special project.'"

"Has he ever been married?"

"Not that I'm aware of, although he could have been back in Switzerland, for all I know. I'm still digesting what you said about him and Irene Bergman."

"I wonder if they're carrying on now."

Rickman shook his head. "I wouldn't have thought he was her type. But then, I never thought Arthur was exactly her type, either, although I always liked him, despite his phlegmatic disposition."

"Just what is her type?"

"Good question," he said before taking a healthy bite of his hamburger. "I would have thought she'd have hooked up with somebody more outgoing than either of them. Both brilliant, yes, without question, but not exactly brimming with personality and charm."

"Yet Bergman, at least, seemed to reel women in like a fisherman in a newly stocked pond," I said.

"Indeed, particularly of the coed variety. I must admit I've never understood that."

"Young women in search of a father figure to comfort them, perhaps?"

"Maybe. It's as good as any other explanation that comes to mind."

"You came in here to get away from campus gossip, and that's essentially all we've been doing," I said with a dry laugh. "Afraid I'm a bad influence."

"Nah, you're a newspaperman. You're allowed to gossip."

"True. We call it 'researching a story.'"

"Well, in any event, I don't think either of us is any more knowledgeable than when we walked in here today," Rickman said as he finished his meal and rose. "Except now I know a little more about the social activities of a living colleague and the ex-spouse of a deceased one."

"I'm not sure I'd call that progress," I told him, leaving a quarter tip on the counter for Chester and taking my check to the cashier. "If you happen to hear anything interesting, I can be reached at the Hyde Park police station, my new office when I'm not in here."

"It's unlikely," Rickman said with a wry grin. "I barely know what's happening in my own department most of the time."

"Well, whatever else you do, stay healthy," I said. "One dead professor is more than enough."

Chapter 17

Desk Sergeant Mark Waldron wore a dour expression when I sauntered into the Hyde Park precinct a few minutes before nine on Tuesday morning.

"Ah, Snap Malek, the phone has been ringing off the hook for you. Your city desk called twice, and also Mr. MacAfee at 11th and State."

"Huh? They know I'm not on the clock until nine. What's their problem?"

"Before you call them back, there's something you should know," the sergeant said, still dour.

"Yes?"

"There has been another murder–another U of C professor."

"I'll be damned. Who?"

"Fellow named Schmid, Dieter Schmid. Found strangled this morning in his apartment over on Dorchester. The big man himself is going to be coming down here."

"Fahey?" Waldron nodded.

I used a police phone to call the paper and got Mulvany, one of the assistant city editors. "Malek!

171

Another prof down on the Midway got knocked off."

"I just heard. I'm at the Hyde Park station."

"Well get yourself over to the scene, pronto." He gave me the address on Dorchester and I told him I was on my way. But first, I called MacAfee. "I hear we've got us another dead faculty man, Al."

"Snap. Yes, I heard about it when I walked into the press room. I've just been down with Fahey, and he's beside himself. Figures the heat's really going to be on the department now. He'll be heading down to Hyde Park shortly."

"Got any details?"

"Not much. This guy, name's Schmid, that's without a 'T', was found this morning by a neighbor. His apartment door was ajar, which was unusual, and the neighbor, a guy named Prescott who was passing by in the hall, called his name and then pushed the door open. He found the body on the kitchen floor with a rope around his neck, looked like clothesline."

"Sounds familiar."

"Indeed. Bet you figured the South beat was going to be a quiet way to spend a few weeks, didn't you?"

"I don't know what I figured, Al. I'm off to the scene."

I briefly looked for a taxi, but ended up walking the six blocks to the brick apartment building on Dorchester north of the campus. Small knots of onlookers huddled together across the street, looking at the building, talking in hushed tones, and gesturing toward the third floor. Two squad cars sat at the curb and a young patrolman stood guard at the entrance. I had apparently beaten any other reporters and photogs to the scene, or else they were inside.

"Malek, *Tribune*," I told the patrolman, flashing my press card and striding toward the door as if I belonged in the building.

Stone-faced, he shook his head and moved to block me. "Nobody goes in," he snapped.

"Fahey here yet?" He shook his head. "Who's upstairs?" Another shake of the head. It became clear that we weren't about to have a chat. I leaned against a tree in the parkway, pulled out my notebook, and scribbled a description of the structure, a typical four-story Chicago-style brick apartment building similar to the one a few blocks away where Arthur Bergman had lived–and died.

A siren grew louder, and an unmarked car roared down the block and lurched to a stop, brakes squealing. Chief of Detectives Fergus Fahey, in black overcoat and homburg, stepped out of the back seat and scowled at me.

"I might have known I'd find you here."

"And a good morning to you as well, Chief."

"Where are your fellow snoops? I expected a crowd," he snarled.

"Beats me, although not everyone is as resourceful

and aggressive as I am. Are we going up?"

Fahey looked at me, then at the patrolman. "I wouldn't let him through, sir," the uniformed cop said stiffly.

"You exercised fine judgment, son. However, I'll take him in with me or else I'd never hear the end of it."

"You are indeed a fine gentleman, Fergus," I told him as we climbed the carpeted stairway to the third floor.

The apartment was jammed with cops and a bespectacled little guy in a brown suit who I recognized as a medical examiner. He was kneeling next to the body, which lay face up on the kitchen's linoleum floor. Schmid was fully clothed, shirt, no tie and open-collared. As with Bergman, there was a cord looped around his neck and sunk deep into the skin. I'll spare you the details and simply report that his facial expression and color were remarkably similar to what I had seen in Bergman's apartment, although thankfully there was no stench. He apparently hadn't been dead long enough for that.

The examiner looked up at Fahey. "Dead at least ten hours, maybe more," he said, answering the chief's unspoken question. "Death appears to be by strangulation. We'll confirm that in the post mortem, of course. No visible bruising, no torn clothing."

Fahey grunted and turned to a detective named Connors, whom I'd met on occasion. "Any indication it was a robbery?"

"Nope. Schmid's pocket watch, Swiss-made and a

dandy, was on his bureau in plain sight. Same with his wallet, with twenty-two bucks in it. I figure the guy must've known his killer, because there were no signs of a struggle, no chairs turned over, apparently no drawers ransacked."

"Prints?"

"Mayer's checking on that," Connors said, nodding in the direction of another plainclothes man, who was dusting for fingerprints.

"What about the guy who found him?"

"Pretty shaken. He's back in his apartment down the hall. I've got Melton there with him."

"Bring him in here."

"I really think you'd be better off talking to him in his place, Chief," Connors said. "He doesn't want to set foot in here again."

Fahey made a sound of disgust and turned to me. "I suppose you want to tag along?"

"You suppose right."

"Down the hall on the right," Connors said. "Number 3-H."

We went down the dimly lit corridor and Fahey rapped his knuckles on the door marked 3-H. It was opened by a detective I assumed to be Melton.

"Hello, Chief. You're here to see Mr. Prescott, right?"

Fahey nodded as we stepped into a dark, musty living room that looked like it hadn't been redecorated since the

Columbian Exposition. A small, bald chap with wire-rimmed glasses sat slumped on a sofa next to an end table. Fahey loomed over him.

"Mr. Prescott?"

The little man, who I guessed was about sixty, looked up with a forlorn expression and nodded slowly.

"I'm Chief of Detectives Fahey," he said, showing his badge. "This is Mr. Malek of the *Tribune*. Do you have any objections to his being here?"

He shook his head, giving us a blank expression.

"I'd like to ask you a few questions," Fahey said.

Prescott shook his head and looked at the floor, as if in a daze. "I've been answering questions for the last hour or more. I don't know what else I can tell you."

"Humor me, Mr. Prescott," Fahey said in a quiet but firm tone, as he sat on the sofa next to the unhappy man. "Tell me how you happened to discover…your neighbor."

"As I told…I forget the policeman's name…I was leaving for work. I'm a clerk at a bank on Fifty-third Street."

"What time was this?"

"About 7:15. I have to start at 8:00, but I always stop for coffee first at a café across the street from the bank. Anyway, I was walking down the hall on my way out when I noticed that Mr. Schmid's door was slightly open."

"And this was out of the ordinary?"

"Yes indeed, people in this building don't as a rule leave their doors open."

"What did you do then?"

"I…called out Mr. Schmid's name, thinking something might be wrong. When I didn't get any answer, I, well, I walked in. But I really wasn't being nosy, I was just trying–"

Fahey held up a palm. "Nobody thinks you were being nosy, Mr. Prescott. Go on."

"Well…I stepped in and called his name again. I looked around the living room and turned toward the kitchen. That's when I saw…when I…" He took a deep breath. "Well, you know what I saw."

"Yes. Did you go into the kitchen?"

"Oh no, no! I ran out of the apartment and came in here to call the police."

"How well did you know Mr. Schmid?"

"Not well at all. He was an extremely quiet gentleman. Oh, we would run into each other in the hall sometimes, or at the mailboxes down in the foyer. We would say hello, and maybe exchange a few words about the weather. He was very proper, very formal. European, German I think. But despite that, he was really quite nice."

"Did he have many visitors?"

"Not that I was aware of. But then, this is a very soundproof building. When your door is closed, you never hear anything from the hallway unless someone is speaking loudly, almost shouting, really."

"And you live alone here?"

He nodded. "I am a widower. When my wife died four years ago, I sold our bungalow and moved in here."

"Had Schmid been here all that time?"

"Yes, yes he had."

"Did you hear anything unusual last night?"

He shook his head. "Nothing. Nothing."

"Do you know anything about Mr. Schmid's work?"

"Just that he taught science at the university. Physics, I believe."

Fahey stood. "Thank you very much, Mr. Prescott. I appreciate your time, and your cooperation. It is possible we may have to talk to you again, but only if it's absolutely necessary."

Prescott stood, somewhat unsteadily, and nodded as we left his flat.

"Not much help," Fahey grumped, "but I didn't expect it." Back in Schmid's flat, where the fingerprinting continued and the body was now draped, the chief looked out onto the street.

"Shit!" he snarled. "There's a whole batch of them out in front." He meant reporters and photographers.

"I did you a favor, do me a favor, Snap," he said. "Take the back way, and get away from here. I don't want the others to know I've given you the edge on them. I have enough trouble without answering gripes from the other papers."

"I'm on my way," I told him. "You can send the others up now." I did duck out via the back stairway and over to the Hyde Park station, where I phoned a story in to the city desk. Then I made one more phone call, which was answered on the third ring.

"Hello, Mrs. Bergman? Steve Malek here."

"Oh, Mr. Malek! I hadn't expected to hear from you again so soon, not that I'm complaining, of course. Do you have any news about Arthur's death?"

"I'd like to come by if I may."

"By all means. I've been at home writing this morning, but I'm ready for a break."

"I'll be there in fifteen minutes," I said, hoping she hadn't turned on her radio to get the news during the last several hours.

I went through the same routine at the Powhatan Apartments as the first time I'd been there. Check in with the man at the desk, who calls Irene Bergman for an okay to go up, and then ride to the tenth floor in the elegant little mirrored elevator with the ever-so-polite Marcus.

"Please come in," Irene said, smiling brightly as she swung the door open. This time she was wearing a fur-trimmed, ivory-colored satin lounging outfit and matching feathered high-heeled mules that allowed a peek at carmine-lacquered toenails. Likely not what a garden-variety author wears while toiling on a manuscript.

After she took my hat and coat we went into the living room. "It's a bit early for a drink, Mr. Malek. Can I get you coffee?"

I declined with thanks and took the chair I had used earlier, while she occupied the same place on the sofa as before. I lit cigarettes for both of us and she took a long drag, considering me through lidded eyes. "So, I assume you have something to report."

"In a way. How well do you know Dieter Schmid?"

She paused at least a heartbeat too long before answering. "I'm interested in why you ask," she said, clearing her throat.

"Reporter's curiosity," I said, keeping my tone light.

"Well, I do happen to know Dieter–Dr. Schmid–although we haven't seen one another recently, not for several months. Now it's my turn to be curious."

"I'm sorry, Mrs. Bergman. I should have come right out with it. Dr. Schmid was found dead in his apartment this morning."

Her hand went to her mouth and her blue eyes widened to circles. "My God! What happened? Was it a heart attack?"

"No. He was strangled, garroted in a manner similar to that of your ex-husband."

"Oh, no! How horrible. Where...where did this happen?"

"His apartment. I believe you know the location."

"I...Mr. Malek, why did you come here to tell me this?" Her shock was giving way to anger and she ground out her half-smoked Chesterfield. "Never mind–I think I know. You wanted to see how I would react."

"Why would I do that?"

She took in air and exhaled it, then repeated the process, hands clenched in her lap. "You knew…somehow…that I was acquainted with Dieter. Didn't you?"

"Yes I knew. It doesn't matter how."

"A campus full of gossips, that's how!" She pulled another cigarette from her sterling silver case, not bothering this time to offer me one, and she lit it herself before I could pull out my Zippo. "So let's see if I can follow your line of reasoning: 'That Irene Bergman, she's an athletic woman, and two men in her life, neither of them particularly robust themselves, have been strangled. Seems to me like more than just a coincidence.' How am I doing, Mr. Malek?"

"Well, I…"

She held up a palm to silence me. "There's only one flaw in your theory, Mister Reporter: What was my motive?"

"Jealousy?"

"That might–just might–explain doing away with my husband, he of the roving eye. In truth, I did feel like wringing his neck sometimes, that is until I decided to live my own life. But it would not explain Dieter's death. I'm not sure how much you know about my relationship with Herr Schmid, but I can tell you this: I walked away from him, not the other way around. Oh, and another thing: I don't know when Dieter was killed, but I assume it was last night. I haven't been out of this building since noon yesterday, and I can prove it. We have a hall man in the lobby and an elevator operator, both on duty twenty-four hours. And the back entrance is locked both from the inside and the outside between 7:00 p.m. and 7:00 a.m." She folded her arms across her chest and glowered. "So, you were testing me. Did I pass?"

"Yes, I'd say so," I said, conscious of the perspiration around my shirt collar.

She sniffed disdainfully. "I suppose the police know about my having had...shall we say a relationship...with Dieter?"

"No, at least not from my lips."

"And why not?"

"It's not my role to do their job for them."

"Bravo! So you were here hoping to get yourself a scoop?"

"I was hoping to find out the truth."

"Did you?"

"I believe I know what *didn't* happen," I said, rising. "Now I am sure you would like me to absent myself from your home."

She looked up and actually smiled. "Part of me is mad as hell about the way you came in here and asked me about Dieter before telling me what happened to him," she said, dangling a mule saucily from the tips of her toes. "But another part of me likes something about you–I can't quite put it into words."

182

"My essential brashness?"

"Well…yes, maybe that's it. Have others used that phrase to describe you?"

"One person did, a long time ago."

"Well, she–it was a she, wasn't it?–had you pretty well pegged, Mr. Malek."

"I go by Steve, or Snap."

"Why Snap?"

"Because of my fondness for snap-brim hats."

"So, Mr. Steve 'Snap' Malek, even if you are something of a heel, I hereby confer upon you the right to call me Irene."

"So noted," I said, bowing.

"I also give you the right to telephone me in the future, if you feel the need."

"Thank you."

"One last thing," she said, getting up and walking toward the closet to get my hat and coat. "Do you think it likely that the police will be contacting me regarding Dieter?"

"If I were a betting man, I would say the odds are long indeed."

"I'm happy to hear that, although of course if they do call, I'm ready for them."

"I'm sure you are," I said with a lopsided grin as I stepped out into the hall.

Chapter 18

Dieter Schmid's murder gave the local press something to sink its collective fangs into. In the minds of editors, two killings easily qualified as a "crime spree," and they were not shy about referring to it as such in their pages.

The tabloid *Times,* not surprisingly, led the way with a banner headline that screamed 2ND PROFESSOR SLAUGHTERED! while Hearst's *Herald American* was close behind with MIDWAY MAYHEM! The other three papers were somewhat more reserved, although each gave the murder its banner head, a rarity during the war.

In addition to extensive coverage of the killing itself, the dailies, the *Tribune* included, worked up sidebar articles about past crimes. These included crimes in and around the Hyde Park area, including the saga of the depraved Herman Mudgett, alias H.H. Holmes, who murdered uncounted women in grisly fashion during the summer run of the Columbian Exposition in 1893, and the Leopold and Loeb thrill killing of 14-year-old Bobby Franks south of the Midway in 1924. Only the oratorical skills of legendary lawyer Clarence Darrow saved that pair of youthful murderers from a trip to the gallows.

As MacAfee had suggested, the heat on the Police Department was intense. "People on and around the University of Chicago campus are living in terror," a *Daily News* editorial intoned. "A great university in the heart of a great city is under siege, held hostage by a killer who for whatever deranged reason has targeted two respected and talented faculty members. Our law enforcement agencies must marshal all of the resources at their disposal to quickly apprehend this criminal and bring him to justice. Time is of the essence!"

The *Tribune* also editorialized, urging that the Police Commissioner assign as many personnel as possible to the case, concluding thusly: "The groves of academe are ideally a peaceful place of reflection, contemplation, and the pursuit of knowledge and wisdom. These ivied enclaves cannot, they must not, be assaulted by such as this nameless, faceless slayer. He has to be stopped, and he has to be stopped immediately. It is that or anarchy."

It was at times like this that I most enjoyed working at Police Headquarters. I missed the banter, the observations, and yes, even the pontification, of my fellow reporters in the press room at 11th and State. The good news, however, was that I was at the scene of the crimes, which promised the possibility of an exclusive story, if and when there was a break in the case. And there had better be a break soon, for the collective mental health of the thousands who were studying, teaching, and toiling on the Midway.

The morning after Schmid's body had been discovered, a call came in to me at the Hyde Park precinct. "I feel like I'm your secretary lately," Mark Waldron said with a sigh as he handed the receiver across the counter to me. It was Nate Lazar.

"I was wondering if you are free for lunch today," the professor said.

"I am, but this time I insist on buying. Is the U.T. up to your standards?"

"It is indeed."

"Do you mind sitting at the bar?"

"Not at all."

Just before noon, I plopped onto what had become my usual stool at the U.T. bar. A somber Lazar slid in next to me a couple of minutes later.

"Well, what do you think?" I posed.

He shook his head. "I really don't know. Everyone is devastated, to say nothing of being terrified. I've never seen the campus like this before."

Chester came by with coffee for each of us. I ordered my hamburger plate and Lazar opted for a steak sandwich.

"Does anybody you've talked to have a theory?" I asked.

"No, not even Theo Ward, who came up with that nonsense the other day about Irene Bergman when we were at Hutchinson Commons."

"Other than Irene, what did Bergman and Schmid have in common?"

Lazar ran a hand across his bushy salt-and-pepper mustache. "Well, all of us–Ward, Rickman, Overby, and me–have been increasingly convinced that both of them had been working under cover at the Met Lab on…whatever is going on over there."

"Do you know of any others who are working at the Met Lab?"

"No."

"And none of you know for sure what's really going on in that lab?"

He sighed. "We don't. As we've been telling you, security is really tight."

"And what about the security and safety of everyone on the campus?"

He laughed. "We're all very concerned about that, of course. For one thing, there are a lot more police cars patrolling the streets around here now."

"I should think so. I called the school's administrative office today, and they told me your president, Hutchins, is sending out a bulletin to be posted in every university building today urging all students and faculty to make sure their doors are locked at night, and that they don't open them to anyone they don't know."

"That's all well and good," Lazar said between sips of his coffee, "except from what we read in the papers, yours

yours included, and hear around campus, both Arthur and Schmid likely knew the man who strangled them."

"So it would seem. The question now is: Who will be targeted next?"

"A grim thought. By the way, I came across something curious yesterday that I haven't mentioned to anyone, which is why I suggested we have lunch."

"I'm all ears."

"Well, as you know, several of the campus buildings have been boarded up and there are armed guards posted in front of them, suggesting some sort of secret activity."

"So I've noticed."

"These are classroom buildings with laboratories in them, which seem like natural places to conduct experiments, correct?"

"Correct. I fail to see where you're going with this."

"Well, there's another building that is boarded up and guarded, and it's not where you would expect to see experimentation going on."

"As I said, you have my full attention."

"Stagg Field."

"The old football stadium?"

Lazar nodded. "I walked by the west side grandstand the other day, and they have an armed guard, a soldier, posted at the entrance gate along Ellis Avenue."

"It's just a deserted grandstand, though, right?"

"Pretty much. But there are some squash courts down underneath the stands, although I'm not sure they are still being used. I don't get over that way very often."

"Seems like an unusual place for scientific goings-on."

"That's what I thought, too," Lazar said as Chester put our sandwiches in front of us. "So I played dumb, said I lived in the neighborhood and was just passing by. And I asked the soldier what was going on inside. He looked at me blankly and shook his head, then said he was just told to stand guard and not let anybody in under any circumstances. I couldn't get another word out of him, even when I brought up the weather."

Just then, something clicked in. "I seem to remember at the funeral that the minister, or whoever the speaker was, said something about Bergman being a big fan of the school's football team," I said.

"Strange as it seems, he was. I think most of the faculty, and probably most of the students as well, didn't really care much when football got dropped here a few years back. But Arthur was an anomaly. He loved going to the games and was bitterly disappointed about the abandonment of the sport."

"That might explain something he said to me at this very bar."

Lazar gave me a blank stare. "Yes?"

"You may remember my telling you that when I voiced concern about how the war was going, he said something to the effect that 'If you knew what I know, you wouldn't be worried about us winning the war.'"

"I do remember. For me, that was one more piece of evidence that Arthur was somehow involved in what I am convinced must be research into a nuclear weapon."

"Well, he said one more thing right after that, when I pressed him as to what he meant. His words were 'At the place where we surrendered…that's where we shall rise again.' Does that suggest anything to you?"

"Typical of Arthur to be so cryptic and mysterious. But I'm afraid I'm not picking up anything from that comment."

"Maybe I'm reading that riddle of his all wrong, but to me it says that 'the place where we surrendered' is Stagg Field, where football is no longer played. And that it also is 'where we will rise again' through the development of some sort of weapon that will win us the war. Which would tend to indicate that some sort of experimentation or research may be going on over at that football stadium."

Lazar made a face. "That's pretty far-fetched, Mr. Malek."

"Agreed. I do have a tendency to let my imagination run away with me sometimes."

"On second thought," Lazar said after a pause of several seconds, "you may be onto something, although I don't know how anyone would ever find out. Things are locked down so tightly around here."

"True. But I think I'll stroll by the field after lunch. Is there going to be a funeral for Schmid?"

"Not here. As I understand it, the body is going to be shipped back to Switzerland after the police are through with it."

"Was there any suspicion–from you or from any of your colleagues–that Schmid might have been a German spy?"

"None whatever. He had been in this country for years, and he hated the Nazis–they apparently had jailed an uncle of his in Germany who is half-Jewish. Also, if I were to guess, I'd say Dieter had a security clearance. I'm almost positive he was part of that Met Lab group, given that we saw so little of him recently."

After we finished eating, I walked over to the campus with Lazar and kept on going west to Stagg Field, which ran from 56th to 57th Street just east of Ellis. As I looked through a low fence at the south end of the stadium, I saw that the field itself was overrun with weeds and encrusted with the remains of a recent light snowfall. The grandstands that rose along both sides on the field were topped with castellated towers looming above like some sort of Gothic amphitheater, and weeds were even growing between cracks in the concrete where the seats once had been. A sad remnant of what years before had been a football powerhouse under the famous coach, Amos Alonzo Stagg.

I walked around to the gated entrance leading to the west grandstand on Ellis and, sure enough, there was a soldier in khakis, standing with his rifle at his side, as if awaiting an inspection.

"Hello, soldier, chilly day to be out here."

"Yes sir." No emotion in the voice, no expression on the young face.

I looked up at the Gothic façade. "You know, years ago, I worked as an usher at football games here. Hard to believe now, but this was a big-time college stadium, with maybe 50,000 in the stands on a Saturday afternoon, to see Chicago play the likes of Michigan and Minnesota."

"Interesting," he said, sounding not at all interested.

"Yes, indeed," I went on, rubbing gloved hands together. "Haven't been back for years, but this place holds great memories for me. Mind if I go in and have a look around, just for old times?"

"Sorry, sir, but it's off-limits to the public."

I raised my eyebrows. "Is that so? Now why would a poor old run-down football stadium be closed to the public? Doesn't make a whole lot of sense, does it?"

"I wouldn't know, sir. Orders, you understand."

As we were talking, three men in overcoats and hats approached the entrance from the north, pulling out badges with their photographs on them. I recognized one from the day I had lunch at Hutchinson Commons–Enrico Fermi.

The soldier looked at the badges and waved all three of them through. "So some people are still using this place, eh?" I posed to the sentry.

"With the proper identification," he said stiffly.

"So I can't even go in and have a peek at the field?"

"No sir."

"All right, soldier. Thanks anyway, and stay warm," I said, tipping my hat and walking south on Ellis.

Chapter 19

The next day, I phoned the city desk from my apartment on North Clark Street, telling them I would be an hour late showing up on my beat because of some family business. They could hardly object, as I had been putting in extra hours on the Hyde Park murders.

My "family business" was actually a stop at Police Headquarters, 11th and State, but then, I thought of several of the people down there as a sort of family. I walked into the press room at 9:15 to a chorus of jeers.

"Well if it isn't old what's-his-name," Packy Farmer brayed. "Back from the wilderness of the South Side."

"Have you come to see how first-class reporters work?" Dirk O'Farrell added.

"No, for that I'd have to go over to the press room at the County Building, or maybe to the City Hall," I shot back. "Mac, are these miscreants treating you okay?" I asked MacAfee.

"Oh yes," he said, standing. "Do you want to use your desk?"

"Sit down. It's your desk now, for as long as you're here. I'm just a visitor passing through."

"Well, since you've been down on the South Side, you have truly made a mess of things," Anson Masters rumbled. "Can't you stop people from killing each other on that damned campus?"

"What are you complaining about, Antsy? Look at all the headlines your paper is getting," I fired back. "And those outraged editorials as well."

"Well, I can tell you that we are loving it," Eddie Metz chimed in.

"Of course you are," Farmer said. "This stuff is just the kind of meat that the *Times* thrives on."

"Well, your own rag hasn't exactly been shy and reserved in its coverage," Metz said, referring to Farmer's *Herald American*. "Particularly that headline, 'Another Ghastly Killing in the Halls of Ivy.'"

"Ah, I cannot begin to tell all of you how much I have missed this warmth and camaraderie," I announced. "But as stimulating as the conversation here is, I fear I must be on my way to faraway places. Mr. MacAfee, would you do me the honor of accompanying me out into the hall?"

Mac nodded and we stepped into the corridor. "This is your turf right now," I told him, "so whatever you say goes. With your permission, I would like to go downstairs and question Fahey about the current status of the Dieter Schmid investigation, and I am happy to have you there with me. What do you think?"

Mac looked at me with those earnest blue eyes of his.

196

"Snap, whatever you want is just fine with me. You were good enough to let me switch beats with you during Flora's pregnancy, so I think you should go down and see Fahey alone. Be warned, though, that he's not in the best of humor these days."

"So what's new?" I replied, heading downstairs.

"Well…a face from the past," Elsie Dugo exclaimed as I entered her anteroom. "What brings you back to our corner of the world?"

"I couldn't stand to go another day without seeing your shining countenance."

"Uh-huh. So my face is shiny, is it?"

"Don't twist my words, you lissome lassie. Is the lord and master at home?"

"Last I looked, he was." She pressed the button on her intercom and told Fahey that "An old friend is here to see you."

"Friend? I don't have any friends," came the squawky reply. "Send whoever it is in."

"Whaddya mean, you don't have any friends?" I said as I strode into Fahey's office. "Who but a friend would bring you a whole pack of Luckies, unopened?" I tossed them onto his blotter.

"Well, I'll be damned. Did the brass at the *Tribune* decide they couldn't do without you here?"

"I'll take that as a thank-you for the smokes. And in answer to the question, I'm still on the South police beat. Just thought that I'd stop by for old times."

197

He tore open the cigarette pack and eyed me dubiously. "To answer the question you haven't asked, but no doubt are about to, there hasn't been a break in the U of C case yet. Or are you here to give *me* some news?"

"Don't I wish."

Fahey lit up and scowled. "There are times when I hate this job, and this is one of them."

"A lot of pressure right now?"

He nodded. "Not only from the press and City Hall, but from the Feds as well."

"FBI?"

Another nod. "Arrogant goddamn bastards. They treat us like a bunch of stupes. Had one of 'em in here yesterday in his goddamn dark suit and dark tie and snap-brim hat–no offense–and he was grilling me about our procedures and how he thought that we could be more efficient. Couldn't understand why we hadn't nailed Bergman's killer. He told me that if we'd gone about this right–whatever that means–we would have caught the murderer and there wouldn't have been a second killing. Prick."

"Did he have any helpful suggestions?"

"Of course not! He told me the Bureau would begin its own investigation, that national security is at issue. Said that Hoover himself is taking a special interest in the matter."

"Just what you need."

"Yeah. God, I hope to hell we find whoever did it,

before those pompous jackasses do."

"Their interest just about clinches what the folks I've talked to down on the Midway have suspected all along."

"Which is?"

"That both Bergman and Schmid were involved in a super-secret research program to develop some sort of weapon, very likely what's called a nuclear one."

"We've heard some similar stuff," Fahey growled. "Myself, I don't know nuclear from nickels, but apparently, this is big, really big."

"That's what I'm told by these wiseheads I've hooked up with. They know something's going on; they're just not sure exactly what it is. And some of them think it's insane to be messing around with dangerous weapons material right in the middle of a city."

"I agree with them on that. Why don't they take whatever it is they're fooling around with and go out in some damn desert?"

"That's something you'd have to ask a guy named Enrico Fermi."

"Who's that?"

"He's the guy who's apparently running these experiments. Famous in science circles, I'm told. Got one of those Nobel Prizes a few years back."

"Well, how wonderful for him," Fahey snapped. "So maybe I should interview him about the killings, eh?"

"Don't you think those friends of yours in the dark suits and snap-brim hats already have?"

The chief scowled. "Of course they have. I was being sarcastic."

"I didn't notice," I said, taking a Lucky out of the pack on Fahey's desk and lighting up. "Well, I'm off to beautiful Hyde Park, land of students and slayings. I'll see if I can find a murderer for you before the FBI does."

"Well for God's sake, be careful," Fahey snarled. "The last thing we need is a third murder down there–and of a newspaperman at that."

"Thanks for your kind thoughts and your solicitousness," I said over my shoulder as I went out into the anteroom and winked at Elsie, who did the same. "Come back again sometime, will ya?" she said.

"With you here, how could I possibly stay away indefinitely?"

"Oh, how I miss that sweet talk. Your young Mr. MacAfee seems like a fine gent, but he is very shy, unlike yourself."

"Haven't I told you that after I was born, they threw away the mold?"

"I do believe you have. Now you take care down there on that South Side, hear?"

"I hear, ma'am. You don't have to worry about me. Before you know it, I'll be back here toiling at my old stand and coming to see you every day."

"I can hardly wait," she said, rolling her dark brown eyes with exaggerated coquetry.

Chapter 20

The first day of December, a Tuesday, was bitterly cold, all the more depressing because winter would not officially start for three more weeks. I felt chilled through after my short walk from the Illinois Central depot at 53rd Street to the Hyde Park police station.

"Can't you crank up the heat in this place?" I asked Sgt. Mark Waldron.

"Now, Snap, you've lived through many a Chicago winter, as have I. And I cannot believe you haven't built up some tolerance over all that spell."

"Some things you never get used to, Mark."

He smiled. "I suppose not. Your paper and all the others certainly have been giving this part of town a lot of ink lately, not that I'm surprised."

"Well, how often do two professors get killed, and in such a short span? How's your boss taking it?" I nodded in the direction of Lieutenant Grady's office. Waldron shrugged. "Pretty much the way you'd expect. He's feeling some of the heat, of course, but most of it is being directed at Headquarters."

"I'll say. I was just in Fahey's office, and he is not

what I would term a happy fellow."

"If you think our good Fergus is feelin' the heat, think what it must be like for the Commissioner in his office up in City Hall. To say nothing of the Mayor himself, our stalwart Mr. Kelly."

"Yeah, they're all taking a pounding from the press. And from the Crime Commission. And it appears that no less than J. Edgar Hoover has also developed an interest in the case."

He raised his eyebrows. "That so? Who'd have thought that our little corner of the world would become so important?"

I spent the rest of the morning phoning the other precincts on the South Side in search of news, and the pickings were pretty slim.

The Gresham station had hauled in a guy accused of bilking little old ladies by claiming to be a termite inspector. He was charging them five bucks to check out their floor joists to see if the little fellows were gnawing at them. The Englewood precinct nailed a prostitute who was working a corner adjoining the local high school. Apparently, some of the students were spending their lunch money on something other than lunch.

I called both of these pieces in to the city desk, then broke for lunch. "This joint is still ten degrees too cold," I said to Waldron as I headed out the door to the University Tavern.

I placed my hamburger order with Chester, and had

been seated at the bar for about five minutes when the natty Edward Rickman came in.

"I was hoping to find you here," he said, settling in next to me.

"Most days that's a pretty good bet. What's new with you?"

"Well, there's some rumblings," he said as Chester put a cup of coffee in front of him.

"Like what."

"I was in my office this morning–actually, it's more of a cubicle, with walls that don't quite reach the ceiling. And I heard a conversation some distance away that wasn't meant for my ears, I'm sure."

"Go on."

"I recognized only one of the voices for sure, a colleague in the department named Foster, who I think is working at least part of the time in the Met Lab. Somebody else, I have no idea who it was, had come into his area, which is three cubicles away from me, and said 'Tomorrow's the day.'"

"What else?"

"That's all–just 'tomorrow's the day, 6:00 p.m.'"

"What do you think it means?"

"That whatever they've been working on in secret is about to crystallize."

"I still don't get it."

"Neither do I, totally," Rickman said, "but I think it's got something to do with developing a nuclear reaction, which is frightening. I know the time, but what I don't know is the place."

I drank coffee and set the cup down, looking at the row of liquor bottles on the back bar. "I think I may know," I told him.

He looked surprised. "Really?"

"Stagg Field."

"What! There are some squash courts down underneath the stands, but I don't think they're being used anymore. The place is deserted."

"Exactly. Sounds like an ideal location for something secret."

"You're just guessing."

"Not entirely. I walked over there yesterday because of something Bergman had said. The place is being guarded by soldiers. I tried without success to talk one of them into letting me inside, and while I was there, three men showed badges and were allowed to go through the gates and on in. One of them was Enrico Fermi."

"I'll be damned!"

"I'd give odds that whatever's going to happen tomorrow at 6:00 p.m. is going to happen somewhere inside that old heap of a stadium."

"You're really something," Rickman said to me in a voice tinged with admiration. "I've been around this collection of Gothic buildings for years, know a lot of people, know where quite a few bodies are buried and where some of the skeletons are, and you've only been around here–what?–a few weeks, and you already know more than I do."

"Just about this one thing," I told him, "and I'm not one-hundred-percent positive about that."

"What are you going to do?" Rickman asked as Chester refilled his cup.

I threw up my hands. "What can I do? Tell the police? It doesn't sound like anything illegal is going on. Tell my newspaper? Hah! If there is a weapon being developed, they're sure as hell not going to print anything about it and reveal some sort of military secret in the process. We got into enough trouble over that Japanese code business, even if we were cleared by the government after an investigation. The Colonel may not be overly fond of F.D.R. and his administration, but he is above all a loyal American."

Rickman stared straight ahead, resting his chin on his hands. "I don't think I want to be anywhere near this campus tomorrow night," he said soberly.

I had my own idea about that.

Wednesday was about as dull as Tuesday as far as my beat was concerned, and the time seemed to drag.

"Seems like you're looking at your watch every ten minutes," Waldron observed after I'd phoned an item to the city desk about a bookie joint raid on South Halsted. "Got yourself a hot date tonight?"

"Not exactly," I said, grinning. "I'm not quite sure

what to call it."

"Well, may you enjoy yourself whatever it is," he said, turning to answer his phone.

At five o'clock, I left the Hyde Park precinct and strolled over to the University Tavern to have a beer. I needed one, and just one, to settle my nerves. Chester apparently had the night off, and an older woman with hair tinged with gray poured me a draught. Most of the stools were empty and she was in a chatty mood, so I became her target.

"Business is slow so far tonight," she said, passing a rag over the surface of the bar. "Maybe people's beginning their Christmas shopping already. Think so?"

"Could be," I allowed. "I won't begin thinking about that for at least another week or so."

"Me too. Anyway, I ain't got that many presents to buy. Husband's dead, daughter in Colorado has just the one kid, my little granddaughter, and that's about it. How 'bout you?"

"Pretty much the same. No wife, teen-aged son."

"No girlfriend?"

"No," I said. "Although there's someone whom I'm getting interested in."

"Well, if you want her to be interested in you as well, you might consider getting her at least a small gift," she said with a chuckle. "It can't hurt, now, can it?"

"You make a good point," I told her, as I ordered

another beer.

It was past 5:30 when I left the U.T. and headed west on 57th Street. The grandstands on the east and west sides of Stagg Field loomed, darker even than the dark skies. But for the moment, it was the lower south end-zone bleachers that interested me. I had noticed on my previous visit that there was a gap in a fence where those end-zone seats almost joined up with the towering east stands. I had a flashlight, but my eyes had adjusted to the darkness well enough that I didn't need to turn it on, not that I would have anyway.

The surface of the old field was uneven and overrun with weeds. Moving toward the west stands, I gingerly picked my way across the broad expanse where the likes of Walter Eckersall and Jay Berwanger once had romped in front of thousands of cheering Maroon fans and where Red Grange had starred for the visiting University of Illinois team.

Halfway up the stands, a series of openings led to tunnels that slanted down toward street level. I knew these well, having ushered several times at one of them near the south end of the stadium. It was to that opening that I went, stepping carefully up the tiers where seats had once been. The opening had been boarded up, but not securely. With some pulling and prying, I was able to pull the plywood board loose, thankfully making almost no noise in the process. I stepped into the darkened tunnel, and was forced to use my flashlight.

The ramp sloped down to a catwalk, and apart from the darkness and lack of humanity, the gray underbelly of the stadium was much as I had remembered it from those festive fall afternoons more than two decades ago. I was glad to have worn soft-soled shoes as I made my way silently along the concrete. I stopped and listened for sounds. Nothing.

Walking farther north under the stands, I played the flashlight back and forth on the catwalk ahead of me. Then I heard something. Conversation? I moved ahead, switching off the light as my eyes gradually adjusted to the darkness.

Yes, it was voices, and they were getting gradually clearer as I moved ahead. Then I saw a sliver of soft amber light slanting across the concrete hallway several yards ahead of me.

The light was coming through a window-like hole about three feet square in the brick wall. I stopped short of it and edged forward slowly. Keeping back from the opening so that I was in the shadows, I looked down into a room that was about two stories high. My opening was at ceiling level, giving me an excellent vantage point.

Slightly below me was a balcony on which about forty people clustered, only one of them a woman. They apparently had been there for some time and were talking quietly among themselves. They all had their backs to me and were looking down onto the floor of the shadowy room, which was about ten feet below them.

The object of their attention was a bulky square column of wooden timbers and what looked like black bricks, which nearly reached the ceiling. The column was enclosed on three sides by a sort of fabric shroud. At the east end of the balcony, four men gathered around what appeared to be a control panel. One of them I recognized as Enrico Fermi.

There was only one man on the floor of the room. "All right, George," Fermi called down to him. "Pull it out another foot." The one called George pulled a rod out of the bulky column. "This is going to do it," Fermi said to the man next to him. "Now it will become self-sustaining. The trace will climb and continue to climb. It will not level off."

Fermi turned away then and started fiddling with a slide rule. After about a minute, he closed it and turned to the onlookers with a smile. "The reaction is self-sustaining," he announced in a quiet but firm tone.

Everyone then grew silent for what seemed like a half hour as Fermi and the others around him watched the controls. Twice I was able to stifle a cough, and my feet were complaining about my having to stand for so long. "Okay, that's it," Fermi said. Soon all those on the balcony were talking and smiling, and then they broke into spontaneous but respectful applause.

One man stepped forward from the little crowd and held out a bottle of Chianti to Fermi. "For you, sir," he said in an accented voice.

"For all of us," Fermi replied, beaming. Quickly, paper cups materialized and the Italian was pouring small portions of the wine into each of them. There was no toast, but when Fermi held up his cup, they all drank to what one man termed "a truly momentous day."

It was obvious that whatever I had witnessed was a success, and that the experiment was over. People began to leave the balcony, talking in excited tones to one another. I walked silently back the way I had entered. My eyes had become accustomed to the darkness, so I had no need of the flashlight.

I picked my way carefully down through the grandstands to the field and headed back southeast. Just as I was about to step through the opening between the east and south stands and onto the 57th Street sidewalk, I saw a movement to my left, but by the time I turned in that direction, it was too late.

Chapter 21

The rope or cord or whatever it was dug into my neck before I realized what was happening. I got the fingers of both hands under it, but the leverage was too great.

"So, Mr. Malek, nosing around where you shouldn't be. A very bad habit."

"You!" I managed in a croaky voice as I tried to break free.

"Reporters!" The voice behind me was disdainful. "Bunch of frustrated gossips, every one of you. Just interested in getting the story, not in anyone or anything else. And not interested in the harm it might do."

"I didn't get any story tonight," I rasped in a voice I barely recognized.

"Whether you did or not is immaterial, because you won't ever be able to write it." With a yank, the cord tightened, and I could feel myself losing consciousness. My assailant was behind me, and my arms were useless, even if I had tried to pull them away from my neck, where the cord was biting into my gloved fingers.

I remember thrashing around, and not much more. I looked down and saw the gray concrete of the sidewalk below just before I was thrown forward violently with a great weight on top of me. I thought I heard a groan, but it might have been me.

It didn't seem like a bed, but it was comfortable, and I had no desire to get up. However a voice, a familiar voice, was insistent. "Come on, Snap, come on." A cup of water was pressed against my lips and I drank, although it hurt like the devil to swallow. I slowly opened my eyes and found myself looking up into the large, ruddy, and indescribably welcome face of one Fergus Sean Fahey.

He was leaning into the back seat of a car, where I was lying. "Thought we might have lost you there for awhile," he said gruffly. "Can you sit up?"

I hurt in about half a dozen different places, including my left cheekbone, which apparently had made contact with the sidewalk, both hands, one leg, and of course my neck. But I was able to lever myself into a sitting position. I peered out into the darkness.

"Where are we?" I whispered.

"You are in the back seat of a cruiser, and we're on 57th Street near Stagg Field. See that fellow there?" He gestured to a young man on the sidewalk talking to a uniformed cop and occasionally looking in my direction with a worried expression.

"What about him?"

"You owe him your life, Snap," Fahey said. "He was

walking along on the other side of 57th and saw what was happening to you. He came up behind the guy and landed hard on him, and then all three of you toppled over onto the walk. Your strangler was in the middle, like a slice of ham in a sandwich, and had the wind knocked out of him. That's when the young guy, he's a junior at the university, kicked him in the balls–hard–and called for help.

"A cruiser got here a few minutes later. The driver knows a little about first aid and checked you out. You were unconscious on the pavement with a cord around your neck. Luckily, it had loosened when you all fell, and our man said he could see that you were going to be okay. I got called at home–I live over in Bridgeport as you know–and it isn't that far away. I've been here maybe twenty or so minutes. That was long enough to talk to someone who's all but confessed to the murders of two professors and the attempt at killing a reporter for the *Chicago Tribune*."

"And just where is our lunatic?" I asked in my still-hoarse voice.

"Right over there, in that squad car on the other side of the street," Fahey said, gesturing with a thick forefinger.

I looked across the street. The dome light was on in that cruiser, and it cast an eerie glow on the profile of Chester, the University Tavern bartender, who was sitting in the back seat with a uniformed officer. His arms were behind him, suggesting that he was cuffed. Those beefy hands had done enough damage.

"Yeah, I recognized the bastard's voice as he was trying to strangle me. But why, Fergus? Why me and why those two profs?"

"He babbled like a goddamn brook, first to the guys in the cruiser and then to me. It was almost like he was glad to be caught."

"Maybe he was. Tell me about it."

Fahey nodded grimly. "As you may know, our man Chester–last name Waggoner–has a son in the Navy. Chester's divorced, by the way. His wife took off years ago and he raised the boy alone. He is absolutely obsessed about the kid getting killed in the war. Sounds like that's all he thinks about."

"So?"

"I'm getting to it," Fahey said. "Being a barkeep, he hears a lot of conversations. People tend to talk in bars, sometimes too much."

"As in 'Loose lips sink ships'?"

"Right, and they tend to forget that the bartender is even there. He becomes like a piece of the furniture. Same way with waiters. It seems that Chester had some idea that an important weapon was being developed down here, and he was all for it. Anything that could win the war for us–and the quicker the better–would bring his son home safely."

"And?"

"And he said Bergman often talked too much about

his work on the weapon when he was in the bar. It really riled him, thought there might be spies around. Felt the prof was endangering security."

"So he killed him?"

"Yep, went to Bergman's apartment, and the guy let him in. Why not? He knew the bartender and didn't have any reason to fear him. Chester doesn't have any remorse at all about it. And this is the same guy who, when one of my men interviewed him right after the murder, praised Bergman as a wonderful fellow."

"Yeah, come to think of it, Chester lauded Bergman to me as well," I told Fahey. "Had me fooled. Then what about Schmid?"

"That's a horse of a different color. Chester had heard some other faculty member in the bar kidding him about being a German."

"I heard about that, too. But he was Swiss."

"Chester didn't think so. He got it into his head that the guy was a Nazi spy."

"Screwy. What about me?"

"Chester has good ears. He heard somebody telling you yesterday that something big was going to happen tonight. And he also heard you talk about Stagg Field, so he put two and two together, got four, and followed you, both to and from the field. He figured you were going to write about whatever had happened in there."

"There was no possible way I could have written about what I saw, even if I understood it."

"Yeah, but this Chester of ours, he didn't know that. He thinks that all newspaper reporters are amoral and are more interested in getting stories than they are patriotic. He was determined that no word was going to get out about the weapon, even though he himself doesn't seem to have any idea what the thing is."

"Nor do I, for that matter, and I actually was present a while ago in a place where I shouldn't have been."

"I don't want to know about it," Fahey snapped.

"That makes two of us. Is the FBI here now?"

The chief allowed himself a brief smile. "No. And I'll call them when I'm good and ready."

Chapter 22

The tricky part was the coverage. The last thing any newspaper reporter wants is to be a part of the story himself. How was the *Tribune* going to write a piece that involved me directly? And how would we tiptoe around the business about the secret weapon?

The next morning, I was ordered to report to the managing editor's office in Tribune Tower. Pat Maloney greeted me cordially, but with reserve.

"Well, Mr. Malek," he said, sitting behind his desk as I took a chair in front of it, "as you know, the police have released very little information on the capture of the Hyde Park murderer, which explains why our story this morning, and the *Sun's* as well, are so brief. I know this man Waggoner, who by the way has confessed to both murders, was caught while trying to strangle you, but I want to know why."

I had decided to make no mention of my trip inside Stagg Field, and since Chester didn't know exactly where I had been or what I had seen, I felt that my visit would never come to light. "I don't know myself, sir. Since I'm the only reporter who has been down in Hyde Park regularly throughout the period when these professors were killed, I can only assume that he felt I was suspicious of him."

"And were you?"

"No, not in the least. But after two murders, he may have become paranoid."

Maloney nodded. "All right," he said, leaning back and looking at the ceiling. "There's going to be a press conference this morning at 11th and State announcing the capture. I assume it will be the Commissioner, as well as Chief Fahey. MacAfee will be covering it for us, and as much as I don't like it when reporters themselves become the news, I think he will have to quote you in his story. Do you agree?"

"I do, sir. I just hope that I'll be mentioned only briefly."

He frowned. "Unfortunately, I don't see how we can do that. After all, you came very close to being Waggoner's third victim, and that is how he was caught. You'll have to give MacAfee some description as to what it felt like, unpleasant as I know that is. Please don't misinterpret what I'm going to say, as I'm extremely happy that you survived a close call. But in one sense, this has been good for the *Tribune*. It shows that we are on the front line in big stories, that our reporters are aggressive."

So that was how it played out. We ran a banner story the next morning, under the headline TRIB REPORTER

SURVIVES ATTACK, KILLER NABBED AT U OF C. I was quoted at length by MacAfee, saying that I knew Chester Waggoner slightly from my visits to the University Tavern, but that I had no idea as to why he would want to kill me, other than that I was a reporter who he may have felt suspected him.

The other papers all played the story big as well, of course, and each of them was forced to run quotes from me, whether they liked it or not.

The most bizarre aspect was that I ended up giving quotes to the very men I had worked with in the Headquarters press room for years: Masters, Farmer, O'Farrell, and Metz, all of whom ragged me unmercifully, both at the time and later. But I got some measure of revenge on them by giving my most colorful comments to Joanie from City News.

Chapter 23

Of course it was not until years later that I understood the full significance of what I had witnessed in the dreary, catacomb-like underbelly of Stagg Field on that historic December day. By then the war was over and I was happily married, living in a comfortable house in Oak Park with a wonderful woman named Catherine, although that is a story for another time.

The war ended just before the military had a chance to draft Peter, who, after graduation from Lake View High–with honors, I might add–entered the University of Illinois in Champaign, where he now is in graduate school in architecture. All those years of constructing bridges and towers with Erector sets had left their impact on him.

I never got around to calling Irene Bergman as she had suggested. My attentions had become focused solely on Catherine. But I did read a review in the *Trib* praising her book about the family in Civil War Maryland. The reviewer said "she shows increasing promise as an author of historical novels. It is to be hoped that she will continue to grow in the genre."

A couple of other loose ends, both of which are worth

mentioning:

First, Scott, the brother of Joanie, our City News Bureau reporter in the Headquarters press room, survived the Bataan Death March. He was released from Japanese captivity when General MacArthur's troops retook the Philippines late in the war. Last I heard, he had married and was raising a family in one of the western suburbs, Maywood I think, a town which had supplied so many of the troops that fought at Bataan.

Second, Alvin MacAfee's wife, Flora, had an uneventful delivery and gave birth to a healthy girl, Rose Ellen, who I am proud to call my goddaughter. Al, no longer the shy and respectful young journalist of earlier days, is now the *Tribune's* City Hall reporter. And in that role, he is something of a bulldog, throwing questions at Mayor Edward J. Kelly that hizzoner would prefer not to answer. I credit this change in Al's personality to his days in the Headquarters press room, where he was forced to spar with the likes of Dirk O'Farrell and Packy Farmer and the redoubtable Anson Masters.

As for Chester Waggoner, he eventually went to the electric chair, and remained unrepentant to the end. He steadfastly refused a lawyer, insisting that both of the men that he killed had endangered national security and were in effect traitors. "God knows without any doubt that I did the right thing," he said to the priest who visited him in his cell on the last day of his life. "I look forward to telling him all about it when I see him in heaven."

Fergus Fahey had his moment of glory in the Waggoner case, getting praise from the Mayor for his "unstinting and tireless dedication to duty in this awful episode." I'm sure he was happy about the accolades, but he was even happier that those accolades went to him and not to the FBI.

Maybe it was my incessant nagging to Maloney, or perhaps it was that he liked the way I handled myself on what I now refer to as the "Hyde Park Affair," but I finally got the opportunity to go to Europe as a correspondent. I worked in the *Trib's* London bureau during the last year of the war, and covered the election in which Clement Attlee defeated Churchill, which shocked many Americans. I also was at the "Big 3" Potsdam conference of Allies, at which Attlee, Truman, and Stalin discussed the shape postwar Europe would take.

It was an exciting and eventful year. I loved London, and I promised Catherine we would go there together some day on one of those big liners from New York. But I was happy to come home and return to Police Headquarters, where you will still find me bantering with my like numbers on the city's other newspapers and giving Fergus Fahey packages of cigarettes in return for the superb coffee brewed by the unfailingly cheerful Elsie Dugo.

Epilogue

The preceding is a work of fiction, and all of its principal characters, institutions, and events, except those listed below, exist solely in the mind of the author. Also, any episodes in which historical figures interact with fictional ones are strictly products of the author's imagination.

The 1942 Chicago Bears became only the second team in National Football League history to go through the regular season undefeated (the first being the 1934 Bears). The 1942 Bears, like their '34 counterparts, lost the championship game, falling to the Washington Redskins 14-6. The Bears exacted revenge the next season, however, defeating the Redskins 41-21 in the 1943 title game.

The Cocoanut Grove Fire in Boston's Bay Village district in November 1942 claimed more than 490 lives, making it the deadliest blaze in U.S. history. The disaster led to a greater emphasis on fire prevention in nightclubs and other public places. Emergency lighting, exit signs, and occupancy capacity signs were widely mandated. Today a hotel occupies the site where the nightclub stood.

Enrico Fermi was awarded a Nobel Prize in 1938 in physics for his work on nuclear processes. He moved to the United States in '38 and was a professor of physics at Columbia University from 1939 to 1942, when he relocated to Chicago and oversaw the first controlled nuclear chain reaction under the Stagg Field grandstands on Dec. 2, 1942. He subsequently played an important part in the development of the atomic bomb. He became an American citizen in 1944. In 1946, he was appointed a professor at the Institute of Nuclear Studies at the University of Chicago, a position he held until his death in 1954 at the age of 53.

Robert Maynard Hutchins was named president of the University of Chicago in 1929 at the age of 30. He served in that position until 1945, revamping the school's approach to academics by putting a greater stress on a liberal education rather than specialization. He also advocated the measurement of achievement through comprehensive examinations rather than by classroom time. He decried nonacademic pursuits, including big-time football, which was abandoned by the school in 1939. He served as the university's chancellor from 1945 to 1951, when he became an associate director of the Ford Foundation. He later headed the Fund for the Republic and founded the Center for the Study of Democratic Institutions to study and discuss a wide range of issues. He died in 1977 at the age of 78.

J. Loy (Pat) Maloney started his *Chicago Tribune* career in 1917 but soon after enlisted in World War I, where he was an aviator serving with Eddie Rickenbacker. After the war, he worked in a succession of reporting and editing positions at the *Tribune* until he became managing editor in 1939 on the death of Bob Lee. He directed the paper's news coverage throughout World War II and into the postwar era, retiring in 1950 for health-related reasons. He died in 1976 at the age of 85.

The Powhatan, where Steve Malek twice visited the beguiling Irene Bergman, is a modernist apartment tower on Chicago's South Side lakeshore near the University of Chicago campus. Designed by Robert De Golyer, completed in 1929, and designated a Chicago landmark in 1993, the 22-story structure is classic example of what since the 1960s has been termed "Art Deco." Even today, the Native American-themed design has the power to entrance visitors: The building's splendid lobbies, elevators, mosaics and other ornamentation make it one of Chicago's most interesting architectural icons.

Eddie Rickenbacker made news in both World Wars. He was a flying ace in the first war, shooting down twenty-six German planes in a two-month period. Although he initially opposed American entry into World War II, once the U.S. was in the war he volunteered his services and became a civilian advisor, reporting to Secretary of War Henry Stimson. In that role, he visited military bases all over the world. He was on one such mission in 1942 when his plane, a B17 bomber, went down in the Pacific off New Guinea. He and six others survived at sea on life rafts for twenty-four days before their rescue. After the war, he returned to Eastern Airlines, which he had operated in the 1930s. Under his leadership, it became a major carrier in the 1950s and '60s. He was chief executive of the airline until 1959 and chairman until 1963. He died in July 1973 at the age of 82.

Stagg Field, the longtime home of the University of Chicago football team, until the school dropped the sport in 1939, was the site of the first self-sustaining controlled nuclear chain reaction. Discerning readers will note that in this story, the author altered the time of the Dec. 2 chain reaction from afternoon, when it occurred, to evening. His defense: "It seemed like it should have happened after dark." The old Gothic-style stadium was razed to make way for the University of Chicago's Regenstein Library, which opened in 1970. The site of the chain reaction is marked by a Henry Miller sculpture, "Nuclear Energy," as well as with plaques commemorating the 1942 scientific breakthrough. A newer and far more modest Stagg Field, northwest of the old stadium's site, has tennis courts and a football field. Decades after dropping out of the Big Ten, the University revived football, although on a far more modest level. The University's NCAA Division III football team now plays such schools as Elmhurst College, Carnegie Mellon University, and Eureka College.

Amos Alonzo Stagg, for whom both Stagg Fields were named, coached the University of Chicago Maroon football teams for forty-one years, from 1892 to 1933, and five times had undefeated teams. Forced by the school to retire at age 70, Stagg then coached at College of the Pacific from 1933 to 1946. From 1947 to 1952, he assisted his son, Amos Alonzo Stagg Jr., as football coach at Susquehanna University. He died in 1965 at age 102.

Leo Szilard, a physicist and molecular biologist who worked with Enrico Fermi on the 1942 nuclear chain reaction, was born in Hungary and worked in Germany until 1933, when he fled to Britain to escape Nazi persecution. He did research in nuclear physics at Oxford University before moving to the U.S. in 1938. He joined the University of Chicago's "Met Lab" project in 1942. He later became opposed to the development of both the atomic bomb and the hydrogen bomb, and founded the Council for Abolishing War. In the 1950s, he was a professor of biophysics at the University of Chicago. He died at 66 in 1964.

Mark Waldron was a longtime desk sergeant at Chicago's Hyde Park police station, which no longer exists. The author, as a City News Bureau reporter at the Hyde Park station in 1959, knew Waldron. Using literary license, he placed the sergeant behind the front counter at Hyde Park several years earlier than actually was the case. Waldron, who never once fired his sidearm in thirty-five years on the force, was injured in 1965 while breaking up a fight between a group of young men. He retired soon after, but not because of his injuries. He learned that one of the youths, who he had almost fired at, was only 17. "If I have to kill a 17-year-old, you can have this job," he told his son. Waldron died at 91 in 2000.

A Brief Chronology of the Atomic Bomb During World War II

January 1942–The Metallurgy Laboratory is established at the University of Chicago to consolidate research on a nuclear chain reaction and on plutonium.

December 2, 1942–Enrico Fermi leads a team of scientists in creating the first controlled nuclear chain reaction under the stands at the University of Chicago's Stagg Field.

January 1943–Land is purchased near Hanford, Wash., for construction of a plutonium-producing nuclear reactor.

February 1943–Construction on a uranium separation plant begins at Oak Ridge, Tenn.

April 1943–The Los Alamos, N.M., National Laboratory opens.

July 16, 1945–The world's first atomic bomb is detonated in the New Mexico desert. The explosion is equal to 18.6 kilotons of TNT.

August 6, 1945–An atomic bomb, "Little Boy," is dropped on Hiroshima, Japan, by an American bomber, the Enola Gay. Approximately 70,000 people are killed instantly. By the end of 1945, the death toll reaches 140,000.

August 9, 1945–Another atomic bomb, "Fat Man," is dropped on the Japanese city of Nagasaki, killing 40,000 instantly. By year's end, another 30,000 are dead. On Aug. 14, the Japanese surrender, ending the combat phase of World War II. The formal surrender takes place on Sept. 2.

BIBLIOGRAPHY

Allardice, Corbin, and Trapnell, Edward R. *The First Reactor*. Washington: U.S. Department of Energy, 1982.

Beyer, Don E. *The Manhattan Project: America Makes the First Atomic Bomb*. New York: Franklin Watts, 1991.

Blow, Michael. *The History of the Atomic Bomb*. New York: American Heritage Publishing Co., 1968.

Fermi, Laura. *Atoms in the Family: My Life with Enrico Fermi*. Chicago: University of Chicago Press, 1995.

Groueff, Stephane. *Manhattan Project: The Untold Story of Making the Atomic Bomb*. Boston: Little Brown & Co., 1967.

Lanouette, William with Szilard, Bela. *Genius in the Shadows: A Biography of Leo Szilard, the Man Behind the Bomb*. New York: Charles Scribner's Sons, 1992.

MacPherson, Malcolm C. *Time Bomb*. New York: E.P. Dutton, 1986.

Wendt, Lloyd. *Chicago Tribune: The Rise of a Great American Newspaper*. Chicago: Rand McNally & Co., 1979.

Meet the author

In his early teens, Robert Goldsborough began reading Rex Stout's Nero Wolfe mysteries. This started when he complained to his mother one summer day that he had "nothing to do." An avid reader of the Wolfe stories, she gave him a magazine serialization, and he became hooked on the adventures of the corpulent Nero and his irreverent sidekick, Archie Goodwin.

Through his school years and beyond, Goldsborough devoured virtually all of the 70-plus Wolfe mysteries. It was during his tenure with the *Chicago Tribune* that the paper printed the obituary of Rex Stout. On reading it, his mother lamented that "Now there won't be any more Nero Wolfe stories."

"There might be *one* more," Goldsborough mused, and began writing an original Wolfe novel for his mother. As a bound typescript, this story, ***Murder in E Minor***, became a Christmas present to her in 1978. For years, that's all the story was–a typescript. But in the mid-'80s, Goldsborough received permission from the Stout estate to publish "E Minor," which appeared as a Bantam hardcover, then paperback. Six more Wolfe novels followed, to favorable reviews.

As much as he enjoyed writing these books, Goldsborough longed to create his own characters, which he has done in ***Three Strikes You're Dead***, set in the gang-ridden Chicago of the late 1930s and narrated by a *Tribune* police reporter.

Goldsborough, a lifelong Chicagoan who has logged 45 years as a writer and editor with the *Tribune* and with marketing journal *Advertising Age*, says it was "Probably inevitable that I would end up using a newspaperman as my protagonist."

www.robertgoldsborough.com

Coming October 2006

From Echelon Press

The Scout Master:
A Prepared Death

A Grace Marsden Mystery

Book Four

*Turn the page for
Chapter One*

Chapter One

The shock-still silence grabbed my attention as no shout could have. Moments before, Robinson Woods had reverberated with the incessant noise only pre-pubescent boys make. I'd been a step mom for only one month, but I'd grown up with four brothers. Throat gripping silence was never golden, rather a violent shade of purple or a bright slash of crimson, but never golden.

Harry and I had arrived at Robinson Woods two hours ahead of the designated pick up time for scouts participating in Troop 265's community service project to clean up the woods. Since meeting Will for the first time last month, Harry had immediately taken to his newly discovered parenthood, unwilling to give up any time he could spend with his son. Our early arrival today marked another 'method to his madness,' as Harry thought he might be able to lend a hand since he'd been a Scout in the U.K.

We'd left the car near the troop trailer and walked into the woods. A few minutes later, deeper into the woods we heard the cheery shouts and yells of the boys, happily scouring the ground for trash and treasure. Then the silence.

"Put it down and move away," Edward Bantonini, the

scout leader commanded. The two boys carefully lowered the hinged box they'd struggled to carry. The thick undercover of leaves accepted the box greedily as its shaped settled into their mass. The appearance of the scouts, carrying the box between them, almost pall bearer style, had caused the abrupt silence.

The youngsters backed away toward the rest of the scouts who'd formed a semi-circle around their leader and the wooden box.

"It's heavy, something is in there," one of the pall bearers reported. His buddy nodded.

The box appeared to be about four feet in length and eighteen inches in width. The leader motioned the group around the other side. The whispers began, questioning the boys. "Where'd you find it? Did you look inside?" They grew silent as their leader knelt before the box.

I already thought of it in terms of 'casket' and now my heart thumped against my ribs in anticipation. Most of me wanted him to call the Forest Preserve Police and turn it over to them, but that tiny part which usually leads me astray, wanted him to open the box right now. Harry moved closer to me. I reached for his hand but he kept moving.

The scout leader stood when he saw Harry approaching. His dark eyes registered recognition and he extended his gloved hand. "Mr. Marsden, right?"

"Yes, Harry Marsden." They shook hands. "My wife, Grace." I smiled at him and his open stare caught me off guard. Sometimes people seeing my lavender colored eyes for the first time stare a little, but his look was riveted to my face. I shifted to stand a little behind Harry who saw the look and stepped up. "Looks like an interesting item." Harry motioned. "Were you thinking of opening it now?"

The boys crept forward, anxious for the answer.

Edward Bantonini's face flushed. "I'd hate to call in the squirrel police to open a box of rocks. On the other hand, I'd hate to open something that could be dangerous or something that would give these guys nightmares."

He showed the same mix of mostly good sense with a modicum of the hastiness. Of course, with Harry on the scene a second man could tip that scale.

It did.

"If your concern is something biological, the box isn't sealed and it's wood. If anything had been in there it would have leaked out by now." Harry brushed the debris from the top and used his handkerchief to clean off the written area. "The sides of the box look rotted enough to have been out here for ten years, but the markings on the top are even older."

Edward read aloud, "Property of the United States Army."

Comments of 'whoa,' 'cool,' and 'awesome' escaped from the scouts' mouths.

"This is a munitions crate from World War II. I don't believe there's any unexploded ordinance inside; maybe a few weapons and possible ammunition, which would be dangerous enough."

The boys stood slack-jaw, staring at Harry. I sensed a bit of showboating for the scout whose cornflower blue-eyed stare never wavered from his face. One of the older boys, a Life Scout according to his insignia, stepped forward from the crowd. "Should I take the troop back to the trailer?"

The boys immediately shouted in protest, many faces turned to Harry as their leader in this adventure.

"That won't be necessary, thank you, Brad. I think Mr. Marsden and I can take a look and determine our course of action."

I pulled a length of yarn from my jacket pocket and braided three inches before identifying the dread pulling at my heart. I didn't want them to open it here, didn't want to run that risk. My thoughts had rejected munitions and headed directly to dead body. Since December, my life gravitated to dead bones with a story to tell. I didn't have a good feeling about this crate. I prayed for guns.

"Those are the conditions. Anyone not clear on that?"

Edward Bantonini took the silence as a 'yes'. I had missed the conditions, but the boys stepped back and tightened the group.

Harry and Edward stood on the far side, their backs to the boys. They pried the lid up at each end, preparing to lift it toward them, and carefully staying to the side. I walked toward the front of the crate. Harry motioned me behind him.

The lid lifted easily and both men held it at a forty-five degree angle to block the boy's view. I held my breath and leaned around Harry to look inside. It wasn't munitions.

Echelon Press

Publishing

Echelon Press Publishing

Celebrating Five Years of

Unique Stories

For

Exceptional Readers

2001 -2006

WWW.ECHELONPRESS.COM